# Justified TEMPTATION

ERIN
LOCKWOOD

## Other Books by Erin Lockwood

*Things You Can't Take*

*All of the Rogers*

*Planning Penelope*

*Angles*

Visit my website at www.erinlockwood.com
Cover Designer: Creation Chamber
Editor and Interior Designer: Jovana Shirley,
Unforeseen Editing, www.unforeseenediting.com



ISBN-13: 978-1718715301

# Disclaimer

*Justified Temptation* contains adult content and is intended for mature audiences. While the use of overly descriptive language is infrequent, the subject matter is targeted at readers over the age of eighteen.

This story is meant to be fun. It is not scientifically or geograph-ically correct. Enjoy!

# 

"I know that *thing* is listening on the other side of that door."

"That *thing* is my wife!" my husband says, striking back at his mother's insult.

My back slides down the flat wooden surface until my bottom hits the low-profile carpet. This two-bedroom suite is over two thousand square feet, but no amount of space in the world could ever be enough for Gwendelyn and me.

It's the same old fight. She calls me a gold-digging hussy, and my husband stands up to his mother—*sort of*—and defends my honor. Nothing changes. She's too stubborn and too stuck-up to realize that my family has a lot of money, too. Not as much as Charles, but enough for her to sound crazy for accusing me of being a gold digger.

"Gold digger." I actually hear the words through the hollow wood door as the same words simultaneously ring in my head.

*I am so sick of hearing this.*

I need to do something to distract myself.

I walk over to the dining table, centered in the main room, just to the left of the bar and foyer. A glass of wine sounds really good right now, but since it's nine in the morning, I'll wait a few hours. At least until Charles is ready to enjoy one with me.

I take off my heavy three-carat emerald-cut engagement ring, leaving only my thin wedding band. The ring is so large and distracting; I can never type with it on. That's something Gwendelyn jumps at the chance to point out—that since I take my ring off, it means I have no emotional attachment to my marriage.

This press release needs to be approved and released before the teacher strike hits the mainstream media. I need to put my personal issues aside and focus on the school crisis that's about to happen back home in New York.

*Crisis* is an understatement. More like catastrophic disaster. If I cannot mediate some sort of agreement between the teachers union and the school district on who will pay for school supplies, there will be hundreds of teacher-less classrooms throughout the city and state. We'll have to suspend the curriculum until this mess is sorted out, and thousands of children won't have a school to go to while their parents work during the day. Not all families can afford on-call nannies or expensive childcare when school is out.

This is a mess for everyone, and my nonprofit organization that benefits the public school system will get caught in the cross fire.

I pound away at my keyboard, drafting a proposed solution and press release. I'm three-quarters of the way through when the suite door finally swings open. Good thing I moved, or my mother-in-law would have stepped over me … or I imagine she would have had the urge to step on me, stabbing me with her pointed heel.

"Oh, look, she can't even bother to wear her engagement ring." Gwendelyn turns back to my husband, who is following close behind. "See, Charles? What did I tell you? The moment you leave the room, that *thing* comes off."

"Are you referring to me again or my engagement ring?" I jump in before my husband has a chance to react.

"Hmph." She grabs her calfskin Hermes purse and slides it up her arm and onto her shoulder. "Well, maybe, once I have a grandchild, you'll see how important it is to be devoted to your *family*. Maybe, once I have a grandchild, you won't feel the need to use Charles's *family* money to go off on one of your escapades."

I can't ignore her overly dramatic use of the word *family*.

Defending myself is pointless. Actually, I feel a slight victory. She conceded to Charles's and my request that I use the family private jet account to get off this island and fly home to do some damage control. As much as she must hate it, she has been a huge help.

"Thank you, Gwendelyn," I honestly and wholeheartedly say to her backside.

She doesn't respond. All I hear is the clack of her stilettos on the marble floor in the foyer, and then the left side of the French doors slam behind her, rattling in its wake.

As soon as her negativity vanishes from the atmosphere, I look up to my husband, bending my neck back to see him standing over me. My head rests on the center of his trousers. He's warm and supportive, physically and emotionally—everything I've always needed.

He smiles down on me. "Your chariot awaits, my dear." He bends down and kisses my lips before standing back up, fully erect, displaying his height, allowing the overhead light to shine directly on his bald head. He *outgrew* his hair, as he always says.

I smile back at him. "I hope that wasn't too painful."

"No more than usual. Although she can't figure out why you would want to take an empty seat over waiting for your own private jet." His lightheartedness floats through the air.

My eyes roll. "I thought she was upset that I was using family money to leave the island. Now, she's upset that I'm not wasting more of it."

My husband just shrugs. "It's always something with her."

Stress returns in the atmosphere. I hate the idea of Charles having to defend me to his mother. I hate that I come between him and his family. And, most of all, I hate that I can't do anything right in her eyes.

"Maybe your mother is right. Maybe it will get better when we have a baby."

Charles glides around and pulls out the chair beside me. Reaching over, he grabs my hand in his. He pulls my knuckles up to his lips. "Everything will be fine, my dear. It will happen." He brings my hand back down to the table. "Are you sure you don't want me to go back with you?"

I scoff. "Your mother would surely kill me. I'm not even sure why she's so mad right now. Does it even cost her anything for me to fill a seat on a flight that's already leaving the island?"

Charles shrugs. "I don't know, but I know money isn't the issue."

"Right, which is why I'm not going to let you miss out on the rest of the festivities."

He smiles and shakes his head, but I know he's not going to fight me on this. I know him too well. He wants to stay. He loves his huge family along with socializing and celebrating—all things wedding.

"My cousin has three hundred fifty people to entertain her, and you don't even want one?" I can hear the humor in his words. "I'm not going to argue, but if you want me with you, I'll come."

"No. Just give my congratulations to Miranda and her new husband." *I can't remember his name.* "Tell her I said yesterday's ceremony was beautiful." I smile, knowing this conversation went exactly how I'd predicted it. "Go down to the brunch. Your mother and cousin probably miss you already. I'm just going to finish up here and take a car to the airport."

"Ten fifteen?"

"Yes," I say, confirming the flight time. "There's one other person on the flight. I hope he doesn't run late. I really need to get back," I mumble to myself as Charles stands up.

I begin typing, and he takes my hand off the keyboard, drawing my focus back to him, and pulls me up out of my seat.

At six-two, he only towers four inches above me. We're both tall. I've always thought it is the perfect fit.

"When will you know?" he asks and then puts his forehead to mine.

Thoughts move down to my belly. We want a baby so badly, but we've had nothing but bad luck for the past six months. I never should have waited so long. We got married at twenty-two, straight out of undergraduate, while we both embarked on our master's degrees at Columbia. After NYU, I wanted to venture out of the state for graduate school, but Charles felt like it was important for us both to stay close to our roots.

It took us six years before the thought of children entered our minds. We've always wanted to have kids, but part of me worries I waited so long because I didn't want the reason we had a baby to be because Gwendelyn had said we *had* to. I wanted to make sure it was our decision, and I wanted to make sure we were ready.

Well, we're ready but no baby yet.

"About two weeks." The thought brings a smile to my face.

How could it have not worked this time? The sole purpose for us having sex last night was to try to make a baby. We did all the right things. I stayed on my back, and then we used my vibrator to make sure I orgasmed and spasmed the sperm in the right direction. It's not the most romantic way to make love, but that's what I read needs to happen to maximize our chances for success.

Charles can read my mind. He knows what I'm thinking. We've been best friends since we were twenty. I've never known another man better, and I don't have any reason to. What we have is nice.

He moves the pad of his thumb across my forehead and kisses the tender spot he just warmed—something he has done since college. I suppose it's our signature kiss.

"Fingers crossed," he whispers.

My sweet, gentle husband.

"Now, I'll leave you to get ready. Make sure you're not the one to be late." He boops my nose with his index finger, making me smile when it bounces off.

But, once he turns, I roll my eyes, knowing he's right. Punctuality has always been an issue with me.

"I wouldn't want the plane to leave without you." He blows me a kiss before saying, "Travel safe, my love."

I kiss my fingertips and blow one back to him. "I will. I'll see you soon."

# Two

"Naomi Devereux?" the man on the tarmac asks.

"Yes, that's me. I only have two bags." I turn and gesture to the black car behind me.

My driver is already in motion, retrieving my luggage from the trunk.

"Okay, we're all ready to go," he shouts over the wind. "So, as soon as you're on the plane …"

He doesn't need to finish his sentence. I get it; I'm late. I should have been here thirty minutes ago. If anyone is aware that I'm late, it's me. Sometimes, I can get so caught up at my computer that I lose track of time. I hate when it disrupts others' schedules.

"I know; I know. I'm sorry."

I secure my Fendi handbag up high on my shoulder. The one Charles bought for me last Christmas. The color is blush pink, muted and sedated. He thought it was elegant and would complement my figure.

My light-brown hair whips around my face in random directions as I stride toward the Hawker 800XP waiting patiently for me to board. It's smaller than the jet we flew in on, but I'm not picky. I'm just grateful for the ride.

I climb the thick steps that come out of the doorway to the plane, trying not to wobble too much on my black Prada pumps. The wind is trying its hardest to push me over. I steady myself by holding the metal handrail and stepping carefully.

I'm on the last step when, suddenly, it hits me. I'm about to leave a gorgeous island, my husband, and a well-needed vacation. *Damn.* I turn and savor one last view of the beautiful Turks and Caicos. I should have enjoyed it more while I was here. I'm not sure when I'll have the chance to visit an island like this again. Charles doesn't care to travel, but his cousin getting married gave us the perfect excuse.

"Ma'am," a feminine voice from inside the aircraft calls to me.

"Yes, of course. I'm sorry." My daydreaming has delayed us moments longer. The rush of calm air refreshes me after I pass the threshold, and my hair, knotted and twisted all over, falls to a rest. "Oh, it's warm in here," I observe audibly and remove the shawl from my shoulders, exposing my sleeveless white blouse. I pat my hair down, trying to calm it into a more attractive mane.

The door shuts behind me as I turn to the blond-wood-and-tan-leather decor of the airplane.

"Huh. *Oh!*" The air in my lungs feels like it's been sucked up into my throat. My hand instinctively runs up to my neck as if I could catch the air myself.

I'm face-to-face with daggers. Fierce and dark eyes stare skin-cutting laser beams in my direction. The man's body is just as tense as his eyes. In his black suit, he crosses his legs just above the knee. His elbows rest evenly on the arms of his leather chair. The only part of him that isn't perfectly symmetrical is his healthy head of hair, combed, parted, and styled to perfection.

"I-I'm so sorry if I kept you waiting," I nervously say.

He's visibly upset, and he shows no change in mood. The way he's staring is making my body prick with uncomfortable vibrations.

I'm almost frozen, not sure how to react or rectify the situation.

"Ma'am, please take a seat. We're ready to take off," the attendant says behind me.

"Please," the man repeats, giving me a slight movement of his left eyebrow, gesturing for me to sit.

"Oh, of course."

Relieved the man has shown some sort of human interaction, I take my seat on the other side of the aisle, facing the opposite direction. I notice his suit isn't black; it's the deepest dark navy blue. Soon after my body hits the clammy leather seat, I feel the two engines purr on each side of the jet.

His eyes redirect down to his phone that's now in the palm of his hand. He's studying the screen, but for a quick moment, they drift over in my direction. I feel the urge to pull at the hem of my pencil skirt and cross my legs together—tightly. Something swirls inside my stomach—discomfort.

*Or maybe it's a baby.*

I place my handbag on the polished table in front of me. Maybe what this man needs is a good icebreaker.

"I'm Naomi." I reach my hand out to him, palm down, hoping I'm presenting myself in the most approachable way.

His eyes move from his phone to my hand, and his lip twitches. I'm not sure if he wants to smile or laugh at me, but he doesn't accept my invitation to shake hands. Instead, he readjusts his position and crosses his other leg over, giving him room to turn more in my direction.

"Fight with your husband?"

I withdraw my offer to shake. "Excuse me?"

His brows move up, and his eyes purposely focus on my other hand lying on my lap. The one with the big rock on it. "Are you running off because you had a fight with your husband?" He elaborates on his question.

Before answering, I look over to his left hand, searching for a similar or opposite conclusion. I spot the platinum band on his fourth finger. "No. I have something important that came up with work." I hesitate before I continue. I'm puzzled as to why this man intimidates me so much. "Is that why you're leaving? A fight with your wife?"

His nostrils flare, and his mood darkens once again. "Work was my *excuse* as well." The way he said that, it was taunting.

"It's not an excuse," I quickly say, defending myself.

The young lady, the flight attendant, taps me on the shoulder and bends at the hips to bring herself even closer to the stranger sitting near me. "We're taking off now. We can make announcements over the intercom if need be. It'll be about three and a half hours until we get to New York. Buckle up, and enjoy the flight."

"Miss, do you mind getting me a club soda once we're in the air?" I ask politely.

She tucks her lips in as if she's holding something back before speaking, "Uh, there is a drink cart near the head of the cabin. Please, help yourself." She straightens and walks away, leaving me confused.

I turn my body to watch the young woman move down the plane. I'm curious. She heads straight into the cockpit, sits in the right seat, and buckles herself in.

The stranger across from me *humphs* loud enough for me to hear him. He wanted me to hear him.

"What?"

"Sexist," is all he says.

*Who the hell does he think he is?*

"Excuse me?"

"I saw the way you looked at her the moment you walked on the plane. You assumed she was a flight attendant." He sets down his phone, laying it on his lap. "In your mind, a woman would be a flight attendant, and only a man would strike you as being the captain." He smirks. "I assume you're as desperate as I am to get back to New York. I hope you don't mind that she won't be serving us; she'll be busy helping the captain fly the plane."

*Fuck.*

Technically, he's right. I did assume that but not because I'm sexist. The circumstances were just peculiar to me. She really did seem like an attendant when I walked onto the plane. I never noticed there wasn't a cocaptain on board.

"I don't care if a man or a woman flies this plane. I'm not sexist," I say, offended by his accusation.

"Of course not," he says and then picks up his phone and buries his attention in it.

I hastily grab a magazine from the basket sitting on the table in front of me. *Vanity Fair.* My eyes wander over, and the stranger is still staring at his phone.

I'm trying to focus on what's in my hands, but this guy is so disturbing to me. I flip through the ads that seem to consume the first twenty-five percent of the publication before the articles begin.

I quickly look over again, and he's still focused on the tiny screen in front of him.

The airplane jolts as it moves forward, alerting us that we're taxiing down the runway, about to take off. It won't be long before we're in the air.

I seem to flip right past every page without really looking at the contents until I find myself balancing the pages in the middle of the magazine.

We're moving faster and faster. I look at the stranger; he's still doing the same thing. I turn and look out the window at everything whizzing past us. We're nearly off the ground.

I try to go back to focusing on my magazine. I can't. I close the papers, creating a slapping sound.

As the plane begins to tip up, I angrily say, "We're taking off. Don't you know you need to turn off your phone?"

I have no idea why I'm so upset. I've always had a theory that phone usage and the signals crossing was just a myth; it couldn't possibly affect the pilot's ability to fly the plane.

He ignores me, so I raise my voice. "Excuse me, *you.* You need to turn off your phone. We're flying."

The stranger furrows his brows and slowly looks up from his device. "Guy," he says.

"What?"

"Guy. My name is Guy Harrington. You can call me Guy." He turns and shows me his screen, exposing a green background with playing cards sprawled across in a horizontal order. "I'm pretty sure solitaire has been approved by the flight crew."

Embarrassment is far from my closest emotion. I feel angry and defensive. This man is an ass. He has been nothing but an ass since I've stepped foot on this plane. It's his fault I've gotten so riled up.

"Well, Guy, it's nice of you to finally introduce yourself."

He tucks his phone back into his inside breast pocket and adjusts himself to cross his legs in my direction. "Do I make you uncomfortable for some reason?"

"Of course not," I spit out.

Again, I feel the urge to tighten my legs together under the table. I do feel uncomfortable, but it's not for the reason he thinks. I'm uncomfortable because, for three hours, I'm stuck on a plane with an asshole.

He narrows his eyes at me. "My misunderstanding," he says sarcastically. "How about an icebreaker? What were you doing on the island? Snorkeling adventure?"

I shake my head. "I'm not the adventurous type. I've never been snorkeling."

"Shame. Some of the best snorkeling in the world is right below us." He points down.

I take in a slow, cleansing, deep breath. He's trying to make nice, and I can easily play along. The worst that can happen is that I'm friendly with a jerk.

"My husband's cousin got married. Miranda is her name."

"Ah, Edward. I work with Edward."

I don't understand. "Who?"

He seems more frustrated than he should. "Edward Sherman. He married your husband's cousin, Miranda. We were there for the same wedding."

*Ah, that's his name.*

I've been so absentminded with this imminent crisis at work, which is now on the verge of exploding in New York, that I didn't focus or enjoy the wedding as much as I should have.

"I'm sorry. I've been distracted the past couple of days. Yes, of course, I was there for Eddy and Miranda's wedding."

Guy observes me in a way that disrupts my comfort and makes my chest feel heavy. I don't like it.

He pulls his phone out of his breast pocket again. "I guess I didn't see you there." He gives his card game his full attention.

Just when I think it's safe, I begin to look away, but his eyes pull in my direction. He doesn't notice that I'm watching him look at me because his eyes are directed at my foot, crossed and hanging out in the aisle, and then they travel up my leg, blatantly passing my knee and continuing up to my …

His eyes make their way just high enough to notice my glare in his peripheral. His ogling is interrupted, and he looks up to my eyes.

"So sorry I've made you uncomfortable again," he says, his words dripping with sarcasm.

I readjust again and point myself toward the window. I gaze at the swiftly passing, vapor-like clouds. "You haven't," I say as I allow myself to breathe into my seat.

I'm just going to ignore this guy.

*Guy*, I say to myself. *What kind of name is that anyway?*

"Naomi." His voice grabs my attention.

Without moving my body, I turn my head in his direction, waiting to hear what he has to say next.

"Relax. You're the one who made us late. The least you can do is get along. I'm not as much of an asshole as you might think."

There was something so joyful in his face when he spoke to me, but I'm not buying it. He's an ass.

*This is going to be a long flight.*

# Three

The wedding was lovely. I'm sure it was nice for everyone to get away. It's hard not to compare it to Charles's and my nuptials. Three-fourths of the guest list were probably the same people. Charles has a large family.

Our wedding was beautiful and had everything a fairy-tale wedding should entail … with one exception—Gwendelyn. It was held at the Devereux estate. Thirty-two acres of perfectly manicured gardens and lawns in Westchester County. A little over three hundred guests and not a dime to spare. Gwendelyn wanted nothing but the best for her only son and soon-to-be daughter-in-law. She never seemed to hate me so much until that afternoon.

With less than two hours until our ceremony began, Charles did it. For the first time—and it wouldn't be the last—he stood up to his mother. He flat-out refused the prenuptial agreement she'd insisted on us signing. The one she threatened everything with. She even said she would put a stop to the whole wedding if we didn't sign it. But Charles said we would just elope, and she would be left to explain to the guests why the bride and groom got married elsewhere. Then, he did the most heroic thing I'd ever witnessed. He tore up the document and threw it into a fire. It was basically a *fuck you* to his mother and her lawyers.

*I love him.*

I might not think of Charles as the traditional definition of romantic, but *that* was romantic to me.

Nobody has ever stood up for me the way he has. I would have signed it if Charles had asked me to, but we trust each other, and we knew we both wanted our marriage to be carried solely on that. A prenuptial agreement just felt too unromantic and suffocating. And, on our wedding day, it wasn't something I wanted to consider.

Some say it's bad luck to see the groom on the day of your wedding, but for me, it was the best luck I could have gotten. Our marriage started off on a very good foot, and we've only grown closer since. I can't say the same for his relationship with his mother.

Of course, she assumed it was all my doing and that I'd somehow made my own threats to force Charles's hand. To her, I'm nothing but a gold-digging hussy. But we know the truth, and that's all that matters. He is mine, and I am his, forever—with no conditions or clauses.

Our wedding day wasn't all bad. I'll never forget the look on Charles's face when he saw me walking toward him in my classic Vera Wang wedding gown. It was the moment I felt like a princess at my own wedding, walking toward my Prince.

When the ceremony was about to come to an end and the minister allowed Charles to kiss his bride, he cupped my face, reached his other long hand up, and rubbed his thumb over the middle of my forehead. He kissed me on my forehead in his special way and then again properly on my mouth.

From that point on, it was nothing but a magical party. My mother even got drunk. She almost never drinks, but the champagne was plentiful, and she was so happy. I've never seen her have so much fun, full of so much joy for her daughter.

When I get back to New York, I need to call her, so we can do lunch. If I go more than a few days without seeing her, I miss her terribly.

I look forward to seeing her caramel-colored hair and green eyes. When we go to lunch or shopping, at least once, someone assumes we're sisters. The only difference between us might be that I'm a little taller. Just thinking of her sweet, prideful, shy smile brings me inner peace.

My Charles and my mommy—that's all I need.

I look down to my belly and lightly run my fingers over it. *And maybe you.*

If I'm half as good a mother as mine, I'll be a great parent.

Let's see … if I conceived last night—and I can't think of any reason to assume we didn't—I think that would put my due date somewhere around the end of May. *A spring baby. How perfect.*

I look over to the stranger, who I now know as Guy, and he's looking pensively out the oval-shaped, thick plastic window to his side. I don't think it would take much to guess that he's a stubborn man, but now that he's keeping to himself, I can't help but observe the stress in his body.

Just as I'm about to drift off to sleep, the plane jolts me awake. It surprises me, and I can't help but allow a squeal to escape my lips. Another smaller jolt soon follows, and I tightly grip the seat arm.

A short, static sound plays over the intercom before I hear that feminine voice again.

"We've reached our cruising altitude. There will be turbulence throughout the flight until we descend. Make sure to keep your seat belt on while you're in your seat."

Her words make me want to grip the arm of the chair tighter than I have been. Something doesn't sit well with me. I have a really bad feeling.

"You don't like to fly?" Guy says from across the aisle.

He distracts me from my sudden uneasiness. I turn his direction and welcome his conversation.

"No. It's fine. I like to travel." I realize I'm facing a new discomfort. The way he looks at me makes me feel nervous. "I'm normally fine with it, but this is a little too rough for me."

A wide, mischievous grin forms across his face, and instantly, I feel foolish for allowing myself to be so vulnerable in front of such a pig. I can see the perverted wheels turning in his head.

"So, you don't like it rough?" he asks. "Somehow, I doubt that."

I roll my eyes and huff out an exasperated breath before turning away.

He begins to laugh. "I'm sorry. I can't help it. You set yourself up for that."

"You don't have to be so juvenile," I retort.

"Don't make yourself such an easy target."

I stand up and begin to scoot myself out from my leather chair and into the aisle.

"Where are you going? Don't go and try to ask the copilot for a drink again. She has better things to do, like fly the plane."

*Just ignore him.*

My aggravation and the plane's turbulence throw me off-balance. I nearly fall, but I catch myself by reaching up and grabbing the rim of the fabric coffered ceiling.

"Ugh, I hate small planes. They're always so much bumpier." I meant to say that to myself, but I projected my comment loud enough for Guy to mistake my words for an invitation to strike back with his.

"Well, I'm sorry we didn't have a larger one waiting for you. Last time I'll allow an empty seat to be filled on one of my reservations," he mumbles loudly for my benefit.

"Fuck you," I quickly spit out to him and storm toward the restroom.

The door closes behind me, and I slam the latch across more aggressively than needed. "Asshole," I say to myself before turning on the faucet and splashing my face with water. To think, I felt sorry for him. That was my moment of weakness. I'm cursed with a sympathy bug.

*I've got enough to worry about. Who cares what this guy thinks of me?*

When I splash the water over my face, the cold liquid refreshes the ugliness I felt seeping in. It resets me. It's what I came into the lavatory for.

There's a loud bang that feels as if it came from underneath me, followed by a violent movement that sends me flying over the compact area. My right leg flies up, and my left hand lands on the toilet lid. As I catch myself, my heart starts racing. I feel like we are plummeting down to the earth from thirty thousand feet above, but the plane soon levels itself.

A loud sucking sound and constant spit-spattering movements keep pulsing me up and down. I have no leverage or bearing in this little room.

*This is some really bad turbulence, unlike anything I've experienced before.*

I need to get back to my seat.

I unlock the door and try to step between each jolt and spasm the plane throws my way. Every movement is a struggle. Gingerly, I take each step down the thin aisle. I hold on to anything within my reach. The overhead, the back of the chair in front of mine.

My eyes meet Guy's.

"I'm sorry," he says.

I can't sense any sarcasm. In fact, he seems remorseful and genuine.

I take a deep breath and try to accept his apology, but I don't want to set myself up for more torment. "What's with the mood swings?" I ask.

He looks away, out the window again. "I've just had a really bad day so far. I'm not sure it's going to get much better when I'm back in New York."

"What—" *Whoa.* I was trying to ask him what happened, but another dropping movement threw off my balance.

I'm about to take the final step to the seat where my purse lies, waiting for me when …

"Ah, oh shit." My body flies to the left, and I land on a firm, absorbing lap.

Sturdy arms grasp on to me, securing me to his body. I crane my neck to face him, so I can apologize and thank him, but the plane keeps moving violently. I sit, stunned, staring into Guy's eyes, paralyzed with worry and uncertainty. I'm asking, pleading, what to do with just my look.

His eyes meet mine, but they're laced with just as much uncertainty. "You'd better get into your seat."

I nod, not knowing if I should be embarrassed from falling on him or worried about the certain urgency I need to bring to my actions. At the first sign of the aircraft's stillness, I jump from his seat and across the aisle into my own. I grab the arms of my chair after throwing my safety belt across my lap and letting the clicking sound ease my tension … but only for a split second.

The turbulence was bad. It had given me no warning. But it could never compare to how horrible the feeling of a falling airplane might be.

My attention is drawn downward where the direction of the cockpit is now facing. I crane my neck and twist my body toward the commotion. The door flies open and bangs against the restroom I was in only moments ago. It bounces off and tries to swing shut, but the woman I mistook for the flight attendant pushes back on it, leaning out of the small control room.

"Tighten your seat belts!" she shouts with a shaky voice. "We have dual engine failure, and we're going to have to try for a water landing. Stay in your seats!" she yells. "Brace for impact!"

Earth feels like it's an endless distance from us, but I know we're heading that direction.

My neck and arms are stretched up with nothing to grab on to but my purse strap that's flying around, and the gravity feels as if it's hammering down on us. It's pulling us down with an uncontrollable force. Snacks from the nearby basket weightlessly float around me in a slow-motion swirl. My purse flies out of my hands, hitting the ceiling of the cabin, and lingers there as the plane continues to fall down. Even my eyes feel like they're pulling up, trying to escape out of my body but instead hide in the back of my head.

Within all the chaos, my body and mind choose to shut down. Darkness. Complete darkness and silence among the noise.

# Four

"Naomi! Naomi!"

I can hear Charles screaming for me, but he sounds different. At first, I only hear his voice echoing in my mind, but then other sounds begin to seep in.

"Naomi!"

It's getting louder. My leg is kicked. It stirs me, and I soak in more chaos.

"Naomi, wake up!"

*That's not Charles.*

I flutter my eyes, trying to force them open when they want to stay shut.

"Holy fuck, Naomi, wake up!" That's Guy's voice—the stranger I just met. He's screaming at me.

*Am I alive? Is this real?*

Blurred shapes bounce back and forth until they come into focus.

"Oh my God! We're still in the air," I finally scream out, realizing we're still alive and the plane hasn't crashed.

"For now, yes," Guy says. "But not for long. We're headed for the ocean. You need to bend over and hug your knees. We're going to hit the water."

"Hug my knees?" I'm so confused. I can hardly grasp on to what he's saying, let alone follow through with it.

My fingers curl into a fist, gripping on to my purse strap that's fallen just next to my lap. I'm so tense and nervous; my knuckles are turning white.

"Naomi!" Guy yells again. "Hug your knees!"

I look across the aisle and see Guy is bent over his own lap, wrapping his arms around his legs. His eyes stare up to me, glaring with warning and desperation.

It hits me—the panic and urgency. "Okay!" I yell to him. I throw my body over myself and my purse, stuffing it between my lap and stomach, and I brace myself for the certain impact we're facing.

*Crash.*

The short neck of the plane hits first and bounces off the water's surface. My body, already hunched over, feels thrown down even deeper into my legs. But then the airplane lifts up, whacking the tail in the water and wiping us up in a violent motion. I tighten my grip under my legs and fight against the force trying to pull my arms apart and up. The tight seat belt cuts into my waistline. It feels like a razor-sharp knife is trying to cut through my clothes and burn through my skin.

My eyes close tightly to shut the disaster out, but then I burst them open. I'd rather see what's coming than be surprised. My eyes immediately meet Guy's staring back at me. He's lying over just as I am, but he's completely honed in and focused on me.

*At least I have something beautiful to look at before I die.*

I want to call out to him and ask him for help, as if he could somehow make this all stop and go away, but the brutal noise is too loud. The sound of parts crashing, breaking, and roughly being tossed around like the ocean's toy is too loud for me to even hear myself think, let alone say something out loud.

The plane bounces twice with a vicious thrash every time it hits the water top, and then the skidding begins. Only for a few seconds, we glide, chopping over the ocean, when something catches the air at the wrong angle.

Something flies right over my left ear, creating a whooping sound. The plane is thrown sideways, and suddenly, I've lost all sense of gravity. I can't tell what's up or what's down anymore. Still, I cradle myself and clench my muscles together, clasping my arms under my legs with a death grip.

We roll three, maybe four times before the violence begins to slow. Something else flies right to my face, but this time, it hits me. I don't know what it was, but it was hard. Something that had been ripped from the aircraft. It hit my head, just above my temple, and it doesn't take long before blood starts dripping down. It tries to curve around and run down my cheek, but gravity overrides its path, and it drips down and drops onto my shoe, soaking into the black material. Another droplet of blood quickly follows, coming faster and faster until it's a thin, steady stream.

I pick up my wounded head and readjust it on top of my kneecap. Maybe applying pressure can stop the bleeding.

The noise and the vicious movements begin to slow. The sound of crashing is replaced with a loud ringing. The ringing siren in my ear gets louder and louder until I pass out. For the second time in about two minutes, I black out and escape this horrible nightmare.

I can feel him grabbing my arm and pulling it up before hoisting the rest of my body over his broad shoulder. My head begins to throb with every step he takes while I'm hanging upside down, sprawled across his back. My purse, still clenched in my hands, slaps across his butt with every struggling movement he makes.

"Would you stop passing out?" Guy's voice screams while I hear water rushing in the front of the plane. He smacks my ass hard enough to wake me up.

New blood surges through me, and I get a second wind. I'm awake and more alert than ever.

I scream, floating in the air. In seconds, I'm flying down. He practically tosses me onto my feet, splashing the wet carpet in the cabin aisle. My purse flies out of my hands and lands in the corner closest to the exit door.

"Move," he demands and scoots me toward the exit door at the front of the plane.

Water is coming in from the front since the jet is tipped forward. I know that, if the cabin fills up with water, it might become impossible to get out of here alive.

I run, panicked to get out of this plane while water begins to rush in faster and faster.

"There's so much water!" I shout.

He grabs my arm aggressively and forcefully. "There's gonna be a lot more after we open this door." He points toward the cockpit. "Go check on the pilots. I'll get this door open if it kills me." Guy doesn't even give me time to react; he shoves me in the direction he wants me to go—further toward the nose of the plane.

I'm prepared to shove the door with my shoulder if it gives me any resistance, but it surprises me and swings right open.

"Oh fuck!" I yell once I catch sight of the two limp bodies.

"What?" Guy screams from a few feet behind me.

I can hear him grunting and straining, trying to get that door open.

I can feel the blood draining out of my face, and my eyes fill with tears.

*No. Not now. I cannot lose it now.*

I fight the emotions that try to take over, but I push them way back in order to stay in control.

"The glass is broken, and the nose of the plane is sinking down. We need to get out of here!" I scream back to him.

"You don't think I'm trying?" he roars with rage.

I only hope that brings him extra strength to get us out of here.

"Are they alive?" he asks.

First, I analyze the woman. Her body is limp across what I would call the dashboard. I'm not sure if her belt was severed or if she didn't have it on, but she was obviously thrown and crashed against the plane's windshield. Her head is completely submerged underwater.

I reach out and try to grab at her body—her shoulder is sticking up close to me—but I only grip her clothes. With her jacket fisted in my hand, I pull until her head is out of the water, which won't last long because more water is gushing in by the second. From a few feet back, it's above my knees now.

I hear a bang and popping sound from behind me.

"Got it!" Guy screams. "Let's get the hell out of this plane!"

"Wait!" I yell back to him.

My fingers go to her neck, checking her pulse. I wait a few seconds but nothing. Her skin is cold, as if the blood underneath immediately left her body after soaking in the Atlantic Ocean.

"She's dead," I cry.

Quickly, I drop the woman's shoulder and reach over to the man on the left side, still buckled and sitting upright in his seat. His head is bleeding, but then again, so is mine, and I'm alive. I throw my fingers onto his neck, and this time, I feel something. A faint but obvious beat is pulsing through him.

"He's alive. He's got a pulse!" I triumphantly announce to Guy, but he doesn't hold the same enthusiasm I do.

"Yeah, well, you won't if you don't get your ass out of here now!"

The water is now at my waist and gaining momentum. I bend down, dipping my chin in the water, and reach for the pilot's seat belt, which are five belts that latch together near his crotch. My fingers fumble around, but eventually, I hook my pointer finger and middle finger on the edge and find the strength to push down hard on the center of the latch. But nothing happens. I need two hands, so I can press down and pull the buckle apart at the same time.

I take a deep breath and submerge my head underwater. Reaching out both hands, I'm able to pull his safety belt apart. It instantly loosens against his body.

When my head comes up out of the water, I can hear Guy screaming at me, but I ignore him. My sole focus is on this man. He's alive. He has a chance. I grab his shoulders with my hands and try to pull him out of his seat.

The water is now up to my breasts and gives me more resistance than I can handle. The pilot is just too heavy for me.

I'm about to give it one more try when I'm tugged and forced backward. Guy's arms overwhelm my body, and the bottom half of me begins to float backward as he pulls me with him.

"No!" I pound my fist on Guy's arm, splashing the water around us. "He's still alive! We can't leave him!"

The further Guy pushes through the water, the few feet toward the hatch door, the less resistance he seems to get, although the water is catching up. It's relentlessly pouring in from all directions now, and the threshold of the door is dipping below the surface.

"Are you trying to kill yourself? Get out there!" He swings my body around and pushes me toward the open door.

There's a large, tarp-like yellow slide inflated, floating vertically to the plane's wing in the water.

"We can't leave him!" I yell again, trying to push past Guy and get back to the cockpit.

But he catches me and doesn't let me pass. His strength easily overrides mine. He grabs me by my shoulders and growls at me. I don't think I've ever seen a man look so angry and brute.

"Get your ass out there now," he spits through his teeth with all the resentment and anger in the world balled up in his words. "I'll be back."

He releases me by throwing my shoulders away from him and turns toward the cockpit door. Satisfied that he's going to try to help, I do as he said and make my way out the threshold of the aircraft and onto the slide that now looks like an inflatable boat. The plane is beginning to pull the floating vessel down into the water with it.

*God, I hope Guy hurries. He's stronger than me. I know he can save the pilot.*

It only takes moments for Guy to appear in the doorway behind me.

"Where is he?" I ask, already knowing the doomed answer.

"He's dead," Guy says and pushes me back, making me fall to the far end of the inflatable raft.

Still standing, Guy bends down and pulls something that was attaching the boat from the doorway. He rips it out with raw animal power. Then, his muscles bulge and strain as he pushes against the plane, and we start to move away.

I lunge at him with my fists flying. "He was alive. He was alive, and you left him."

Guy grabs my shoulders and shakes me. "He was dead. He was completely underwater by the time I got back there. There was no way I could have gotten him out, and he wasn't breathing. He was dead," he repeats.

"No." I keep swinging my arms at him, trying desperately and failing miserably to hurt him. "He was alive. I felt his pulse."

He grabs my arms, pinning them to my sides, and wraps his around mine. His body forces so much pressure onto my thin frame that I have no choice but to stop struggling. I can't move anymore, and I can't fight either. I give up. Explosive tears begin to roll out of me as I begin to cry. My body goes weak, and Guy guides me to rest on the floor of the raft with him.

My sobs pour out as I watch the last glimpse of the private plane we were just flying on disappear beneath the ocean's surface. Guy's hand moves up to my head, cupping it with tense consolation.

He's breathing hard. If I couldn't hear his heartbeat pounding against my chest, I might assume I'd drowned with the plane and the pilots. But I didn't. I can feel, and I can hear.

After all the noise, yelling, and chaos, the silence we're now experiencing screams volumes. There is nothing left but water. In every direction, there's only water and the horizon that appears to go on forever.

"Now what?" I breathe between sobs.

# Five

"You're bleeding." His voice trickles into my mind.

I was trying to be somewhere else. Or at least float toward somewhere else other than more water. I was trying to imagine the sound of a helicopter. I know what the whopping blades of a helicopter sound like when it's hovering over ground, but I wonder if it would sound different over water.

His arms are still wrapped around me. I'm not sure how much time has gone by since the silence kicked in, but we haven't moved. I push back against his chest, giving myself space from him. The imminent rush of my life being in danger has disappeared.

"You're bleeding," he says again.

My fingers reach up and feel the wetness above my temple. "I know. Something hit me while we were crashing." I bring my hand down into my eyesight and pinch the bright red blood on my thumb and pointer, smudging it between the two fingers. *What the hell? It's not a fashion show out here.* I wipe it on my skirt, something I normally would never do. But, under the circumstances, I think there are several things I would normally never do.

Life is put in perspective after survival mode takes over. I just need to hold it together and do whatever it takes to survive long enough for us to be rescued. As soon as Charles hears about the crash, I'm sure he'll stop at nothing until I'm found.

Guy points behind me. "Hand me that first aid kit. We'll see what's in there."

*First aid kit?*

"How on earth did a first aid kit get here?" I ask, doing a double take, looking around at all the items sprawled across the raft.

Amid all the chaos, I didn't notice there was anything in here. There's a blanket, a few granola bars from the basket that sat on the table in front of me, a white metal box with a red cross on it, and …

"My purse!" I squeal, falling back behind me and reaching for it.

"While you were trying to kill us by staying on the plane, I grabbed what I could and threw it on here."

He looks at me, annoyed by my actions. I'm frantically trying to open my purse, so I can dig through the contents.

"Your money won't do you any good out here. What are you looking for?"

"My phone," I quickly answer while my fingers dive in and move around, searching for that familiar touch. I pull a full water bottle out of my way and let it drop to the floor. "Ah, yes!" I've got it. I hold it up and show Guy my success.

He doesn't seem to care. In fact, he looks outright pissed. His face winces. "Are you fucking serious?" He grabs it out of my hand.

"What the hell is your problem?" I try to swipe it back, but his reflexes are too fast.

"Do you really think your phone will work after soaking in the Atlantic?"

"We have to try," I plead and shriek. "Give it back to me. It's worth a try."

"Look around!"

I do as he said, out of breath from trying to grab my phone back from his possession.

"Look," he continues. "Do you see any cell phone towers? First, your phone is dead and broken. See?" He moves his finger to the On button centered at the bottom. Nothing. "Second, even if it were in working order, there is no fucking cell service in the middle of the ocean. It's useless."

He tosses it over his shoulder. The tiny splashing sound it makes when it hits the water sounds like the end of my hope.

Just as quickly as he tossed my dream to be rescued, he grabs the water bottle from the raft floor. "Now, this will be useful."

It acts completely on its own, like a trained reflex. Although my psyche doesn't argue with it, my hand lifts and swings, palm up, until it hits the warm, smooth surface of Guy's face.

That slapping sound feels a lot better to my ears than the sound of my phone plunging into the ocean. It feels good.

Stunned, Guy just freezes. His head tilts slightly, and he says, "I guess you do have a little fight in you after all."

I give up. I lean back and rest myself further away from him—as far as one can get on a four-by-eight raft. "Why are you such an asshole?" I ask quietly, but I know he can hear me. I'm the only sound in the world. "How can you go from holding me and consoling me to *this* ugliness?"

He takes a deep breath and composes himself before calmly replying, "I'm not an asshole. I'm just angry." He rests his back arm on the large, inflated rim of the boat. "I don't want to be here with you. I don't want to have to feel responsible for you, but it doesn't mean I want to see you hurt or killed."

I look away from him and rest my cheek on the side of the boat, allowing my body to bob up and down with the motion of the water. "You think I want to be here with *you*? I should be with my husband. You should be with your wife. We should be with our families, not stranded here. But that doesn't mean I'm going to act like a bitch and try to make life difficult for you. Don't you think we're in a hard enough situation as it is?"

Guy doesn't respond right away.

"Your bleeding stopped," is all he eventually says.

We sat in silence for hours, calming our fears and anger. The sun started to beat down on us, so Guy unfolded a canopy top that was attached to the raft. He moved as if he'd done this before.

I'm grateful for the shade and feeling much less emotional now. "How do you know what to do?" I ask him.

"Is this your first plane crash?" he jokes.

I give him a light smile. "I just mean, you knew I should hug my knees when we were going down, and you knew where the raft was on the plane, the first aid kit, the canopy."

He shrugs. "I'm a bit of an adventurer. I've been through quite a few safety and emergency procedures."

"What kind of adventures have you been on?"

"Nothing crazy. Rafting excursions, airplane lessons, skydiving, hang gliding, climbing Everest." He seems excited to tell me, "But only to Base Camp Two. A storm came in that made it too dangerous for us to summit. We had to go back down. But I plan to go back, so I can reach the top."

"Wow, that all sounds crazy," I say, astonished by his experiences. "I've never done anything like that. I've never even driven a car."

He shakes his head. "You've survived a plane crash. I'd say that's quite an accomplishment."

"Survived?" I question. "Let's hope it stays that way. So, do you know why it crashed?"

"I wasn't in the cockpit, and I didn't see the equipment, so it's hard to say. I don't know why we had engine failure, but I hope we live long enough to figure it out."

I somberly nod and look out onto the never-ending ocean around us. "If we don't starve to death."

Guy sits up straighter. "Here's what we're going to do."

He goes on to dictate how much food and water we'll eat and drink and when. I don't argue. I'm saving my strength for much more dire circumstances. Plus, there is no question in my mind that this man wants to survive. And, for some reason, he cares about me surviving, too.

My body is forced to bob up and down with the subtle motion of the sea. My breakfast, not fully digested yet, rolls in my stomach. I just wish I could stay still and stop moving and rolling up and down just for a moment. I would feel so much better.

"You don't look so good," Guy says across from me.

I shake my head, fully rested on the rim of the boat. "I think I'm going to be sick. Maybe I need to eat something to calm my stomach."

"No," he quickly says. "We can't waste food if you're just going to throw it up. We need to make it last as long as it can."

I have been on plenty of large boats. This isn't my first rodeo, so to speak. "I'm not going to throw up. I've never been seasick before."

Guy scoffs. "I bet you've also never been stranded on an inflatable raft in the middle of the ocean. Yachts are a lot different than what we're experiencing now."

Just when I'm about to argue with him, the feeling in my stomach moves up into my throat.

"Not in the boat!" he yells. "Lean over."

*Insensitive prick.*

I grab the edge and allow my head to hover over the water. My stomach contracts, and the contents lurch out. Guy scoots over closer to me, and his fingers whisk my rough hairs away from my face. He bunches my mane in his hands behind my head.

I take a moment after it's all out. I'm out of breath from expelling more than I thought I had in me. "I actually feel better now."

"You'll get used to it. How about an early dinner? We can split this granola bar." He hands me the full water bottle. "Here, just a few sips."

Honestly, by the way he's taking care of me, I really can't tell if he's an asshole or not.

I wish I knew something about astronomy. I wish, somehow, the stars could help us and guide us somewhere. Even if we can't be rescued right away, I wish we could drift someplace safer than the middle of the ocean. The sky seems clear now, but there's no telling what kind of weather will come.

I'm looking at the stars in a new light. "They're so bright, and there are so many of them."

Guy is lying down next to me, facing the dark sky.

"I guess that's the downside of New York City. You can't see the stars like this."

"I've never realized there's a downside of New York. There's nothing better than the Big Apple. You can do anything there. As a kid, I felt like the ultimate adventure was to be a New Yorker."

The motion of our bodies rolls in unison. The calmness of the ocean matches the calmness of the stars. It's easy to reflect when it's so quiet.

"I've lived in New York my whole life. I've traveled, but I've never really experienced anything else. I've always wondered what it would have been like to grow up in a simple, suburban neighborhood." My hand, resting at my side, slides up and settles on my belly. "I think, when Charles and I have kids, we'll probably move out of the city."

"Is that your husband? Charles?"

"Yes," I simply answer. I listen to our breathing, in and out, serene like our surroundings. "What's your wife's name?"

Guy doesn't answer—at least, not for a long time. "Marina. My wife's name is Marina Cary."

I turn on my side. Even though I can't see him very well, I want to face him. "You're shitting me. The model? Marina Cary, the model, is your wife?"

"Yep," he says, only turning his head in my direction.

"Wow. She's gorgeous."

I can barely make out the whites in his eyes against this dark night, but I can tell they're scanning me.

"We finally agreed on our divorce terms this morning." His words are so dry and emotionless.

*Poor guy*. I guess this explains the mood swings—at least, some of them.

"I'm so sorry. Why?"

He sharply breathes in. "We'd been going back and forth for months. But I always had the upper hand. She finally gave up."

"How could you have an upper hand on your wife? Didn't you own everything together?"

"Ha," he scoffs. "I owned my Manhattan apartment and summer home in Montauk before we were married. Not to mention, my business, which she could never touch," he adds. "It's all ironed out in our prenup. She's not getting much, and that still pisses me off."

"She's a famous model. Doesn't she have plenty of money on her own?"

"Some. But she wants what she can't have—*my money*."

I can't help but think of how grateful I am that Charles and I never argue about money. We never argue about anything.

"Especially," Guy continues, "after she slept with …" His voice trails off. "No, that bitch won't get one dime."

"Sorry," I say again quietly.

That sounds so awful. I can't imagine what I would do if Charles ever cheated on me. The thought has never really crossed my mind. We are so close and devoted to each other.

"Don't be. We're both getting what we deserve. We used each other and got married for the wrong reasons."

"Still," I say, shocked, "there is no excuse for infidelity. Cheating is wrong under every circumstance. I don't care how you treated her or not treated her; she should have handled it another way."

"People cheat." He turns his face back up to the sky.

I roll onto my back and do the same. "No, they don't." I get the last word in before enough silence takes over for us to get some rest.

# *Six*

I don't even have the strength to be sick again. It's been three days, and we haven't heard so much as a plane overhead, looking for us. We have one bag of potato chips, a package of six sandwich cookies, and only a few sips of water. I feel as if my insides are eating me alive. Portioning out the food and water has worked so far, but the lack of sufficient amounts of water is the worst. This isn't even surviving. It feels more like dying slowly.

Guy seems weaker, too. It's only been a few days, so he doesn't seem to be much skinnier. His muscles are still defined and swollen with mass, but his energy is low, and the color has drained from his skin.

It's hot. And, if it wasn't for the canopy, the sun would be blistering our skin. But then, at night, the cool breeze off the water makes us freezing cold.

We've been sleeping close together to stay warm and laying his coat across both of us as best we can. This morning, I woke up with my head on his chest and his arm around me. It was nice and comforting, considering the situation, but it's not what I want. It's not what I'm used to. I want Charles. I'd give anything to let him know I'm alive and that I need to be with *him.*

Waking up on Guy's chest made me think about the last night I'd spent with my husband—the hours of cuddling we did after we made love, trying to make a baby. I bring my hand up from my side and rest it on the top of my tummy. We need to get rescued and fast.

"Why hasn't anyone come to look for us?" I ask with a raspy voice. My throat is dry from dehydration and beginning to burn from the friction when I talk.

Guy just slowly shakes his head back and forth. "We're in the middle of the ocean. They don't know where we crashed or if we survived. From what you say about your husband and his family, I'm sure they're looking for us; they just don't know where to start."

I try to smile at the mention of my husband and his family, but I can't get my mouth to fully move. "I don't know. I know my husband is worried sick and probably going crazy." I can't help but let a tear escape and travel down my cheek. "But I bet his mother is throwing a party." I look directly over at Guy. "Celebrating," I clarify.

"So, you don't get along with the Devereux matriarch?"

"No. She doesn't care for me." I shake my head. "What about you? I'm sure your wife is doing everything she can to find you."

"Hmph," he scoffs. "My wife is likely helping your mother-in-law throw that party. Marina will probably bring a date."

For some reason, that makes me smile. Only because Guy said it in such a lighthearted way, I feel no pity, only humor.

I look up and show him my grin. "I know you're joking. You two might have had your problems, but I'm sure she's devastated that you're missing. There has to be some love there somewhere."

"No, she'd be happy if I never came home," he says matter-of-factly. "There was never any love in our marriage; it was more about image and lifestyle."

I look further into Guy's eyes. He can't be serious about what he just said. Marriage is a sanctity that needs to be cherished. But perhaps that's why their marriage didn't work.

"Maybe that's why she left you."

Guy's eyes turn cold and harsh. I've hit a hot button.

"I didn't mean it like that," I quickly say, trying to rectify the damage I've obviously caused. "I just mean that, if you're saying love wasn't in the marriage to begin with, then that could be why she strayed and why she's leaving you."

"Trust me," he growls with a strained tone, "she had everything she wanted."

"Obviously not," I mumble to myself.

Guy leans in toward me. "What?"

"Nothing," I say, hoping the subject changes.

"You must think you have a perfect marriage, so you get to judge mine?" he asks angrily. "Everyone wants something out of a relationship. I gave her exactly what she wanted. Now, she wants what isn't hers, and she doesn't deserve it."

"You're right," I fire back. "People do get something out of relationships. I want love and companionship, and that's what I have. So, yes, to answer your rude assumption, I do think I have a perfect marriage."

His face strains with discomfort. "If it's so perfect, why are you here instead of with him now? Why were you leaving when he was staying?"

"That's none of your …" I begin to defend myself when I realize how alone I feel. I'm arguing with someone, but I'm completely alone out here. I have nothing to lose and nothing to hide. "I told you before; I was leaving because I had an emergency with work. I thought it was the end of the world, but of course, now, it doesn't matter anymore."

"And what's that?"

"What do you mean? What's what?"

"Your work? What do you do? I find it hard to imagine that a Devereux would need a job."

I consider his words. He's right. "No, I don't need a job. But I don't feel right about doing nothing. A lot of people don't have it as easy as I've always had it. I grew up with a silver spoon in my mouth and had the best education provided for me. All so I could grow up to be as wealthy of an adult as I was the day I was born. I had every opportunity given to me, and nobody expected me to do anything with it. There are kids out there with potential."

"So, what do you do?" Guy asks again, seeming more interested.

"I started a nonprofit organization that aids the public school system. We help with after-school programs, enrichment programs, field trips, sports, music, mentoring. We have our hands in a lot of hats."

"Why?" he simply asks.

"Because less wealthy families deserve a chance to give their kids a good education. It's supposed to be free education. But only rich people seem to get it easily. I'm just trying to help even the score."

Guy gives me a strange look. "Where have you been all my life?" he says quietly.

A breeze hits my face and blows my hair behind me. The raft seems to bounce like a baby testing their legs before taking their first step. I push myself up to change position and sit on the other side of the craft. The boat wobbles with my movements, and I lose my balance. I start to fall over, but Guy grabs ahold of me.

"Are you okay?" he asks.

I nod while he still holds on to my arm. "I'm just uncomfortable. My legs are starting to cramp from sitting in the same position for so long."

Guy takes a deep sigh and hands me the water bottle. "Here. Drink the last of the water."

"But then it'll all be gone." I don't understand why he would tell me to drink it. It's all we have.

He disapprovingly looks at me. "Yes, Einstein, it will be all gone. You obviously need it more than I do, and if one of us is going to die from dehydration, I'd rather that happen after the water is all gone, not before. Otherwise, I might look like a selfish ass." He shakes the water in my face, impatiently waiting for me to take it from him.

I snatch the bottle out of his hand. I have the urge to slap his smart mouth again. "Fine." I hastily chug the few sips as if there were an endless supply. I'm wildly disappointed but still relieved from the little hydration I get.

Out of breath from my desperation to quench my thirst, I ask Guy, "How can you do something so thoughtful and act like such a dickhead about it?"

Guy smirks, trying not to smile. "I'm just trying to push your buttons," he says, seeming amused.

He reaches over and grabs one of my legs. I flinch, but it doesn't stop his movements. After grabbing my other leg, he gives me a devious grin, placing both of my legs on his lap. "I like to keep people on their toes," he says while pinching the muscle in my big toe and pulling up.

A small rush of blood revives my foot as he continues to knead and massage my aching muscles. I want to stop him. I want to tell him I'm not comfortable with him touching me, but I can't deny myself. This is the best feeling I've had in over three days.

His hands and movements make me feel things in my body, not just my feet. The guilt begins to seep in, but I suppress it.

I can see his eyes move their focus from my feet up to my knees. His hands follow, and he massages my calf. My heart begins to race, and blood circulates through my body as if I've just gotten a jump-start. I feel alive again.

Guy is so focused on my legs, as if they were a sacred possession of his. He moves his eyes up to mine and shoots daggers into me like the first moment I met him. Just like that moment, I feel as if my breath jumps into my throat. As he's looking into my eyes, his hand moves up past my knee and toys with passing the hem of my skirt. I feel a throb pulse between my legs.

*This isn't right.*

"G-guy." I move my legs away from his hands. "No, Guy. I-I ca—" My thoughts are distracted by what I see behind his head in the distance. I sit up straight and take a better look before alerting Guy of the imminent danger I see coming toward us.

He rolls his eyes. "Naomi, don't be such—"

"No," I interrupt him and throw my finger in the air, pointing behind him. "Look. What the hell is that?"

Guy quickly turns his head. "Oh fuck."

There is a huge storm in the distance, and the atmosphere-swallowing slate clouds are heading straight toward us. I can see the deluge of rain. It's like a sheer black curtain.

"Fuck," Guy says, moving his head back and forth, thinking.

"What do we do?" I want to panic, but I don't have the space. I'm too cramped to panic. I need to stay focused.

He grabs his hair, his fingers straining around his scalp. "We need to get away from it."

"How?"

Guy yanks his hands down and screams, "I don't know!" The veins in his neck are bulging with thick, stubborn blood.

Then, I see an idea hits him. Suddenly, he's motivated and taking action.

He grabs my hand and forcefully throws it overboard, allowing it to slap the water. "Paddle," he simply orders.

I look over to the other side of the boat, and Guy is violently paddling with his strong left arm.

"Come on!" he yells at me.

The wind picks up again and whacks the raft into sharp, little waves forming in the ocean. The once-calm sea is now growing with strength and anger. The sun disappears behind a haze of a dark gray storm charging toward us. The sky is mean and ominous.

I start to paddle along with Guy, but it seems pointless. We're not going anywhere, and I'm not even sure where we're supposed to be going. I trust Guy. At this point, I have no choice; he's all I've got. I'm paddling madly, following his orders.

"This isn't working!" I shout while attempting to control our drifting movements. "Where are we supposed to go?"

"There," he answers, sitting up straight and pointing off into the distance.

A light sprinkle dusts my face and begins to spray my dingy white blouse. I squint and strain my eyes to see far off where Guy is pointing.

I see it. "Ah!" I scream. "Thank God! Land!"

"Don't thank anybody yet. Paddle!"

I quickly move and get to work. My already-wet face gets even wetter when my rapid slapping and swatting actions splash water up, and it covers me.

I don't stop moving. "I'm trying, but this isn't working."

We're going nowhere.

Guy stops and sits back on his heels. "I know." He pauses only for a moment until he springs into action. He leans back and grabs the edge of the canopy, ripping it up and detaching it from the raft. "Here, we'll use the wind."

His hands work like a nimble elf despite their large size. He rips off a portion of the bottom of his pants on each leg. He ties and twists and props the canopy, spreading it across the front of the floating raft, securing it to the small handles that sit on the top rim.

A gust of wind flies by my face and pushes us faster than we were moving before. I frantically paddle, trying to steer our way to the small island in the distance.

# Seven

We're about five hundred feet from the shore when our boat flips over, tossed by a violent and relentless wave. I reach and grab for anything, but I come up empty, except for the thin strap of my purse. It's something. I grasp on to it as if it could save me while my whole body rushes under the water and wildly swirls around.

*Where is up? Where is down?*

My head is still spinning. I'm not sure what to do or which direction to go. Moments without air pass by like hours. I'm about to snap out of it and panic my way somewhere, anywhere, when my arm is grabbed.

It's Guy, and he's pulling me up.

*Yes, this is up.* I begin to kick and climb to the surface with my hand still on my purse.

When our heads finally pop up above water, I gasp, but the rush into my lungs is filled with insecurity and false hope. No amount of air seems to be enough for a couple of breaths. I'm inhaling so desperately that it doesn't feel like oxygen can possibly fit and fill inside me.

The rain is crashing down on us so hard; I can hardly see in front of me. It feels as if it wants to push me back down underwater.

I throw my crossbody purse strap over my head and follow Guy's lead. His mouth is gaping open, his eyes wild with survival instincts, but I can't hear a thing over the rain and thrashing ocean. He is my shepherd, and I'll go with him anywhere, blind and deaf. He's my only hope.

He gestures with his head, and I ready myself to go where he tells me. His strong arms reach above and dig through the water, thrusting himself forward with each stroke. We swim almost two hundred feet closer to shore.

I was on a high school swim team at my academy, but once I graduated, I stopped. I haven't even swum for fun since I was a teenager. It came back to me as soon as we started moving, but my lack of endurance is leaving my arms and legs burning from the exercise. I feel as if I need to rest, but that's not an option here. My purse adds even more resistance under the water. It fights against me moving forward, but I try to push through it with the little strength I have left.

Guy's eyes open wider than what I imagine is comfortable for him. He points down and mouths, *Go under.*

I quickly take action after him. The water washes around us in white bubbles as a wave crashes down above us. I'm only a few feet behind Guy, but something grabs me, and a force pulls me back.

I paddle wildly in the water, but the undertow drags me farther than where I want to be. I can't pull up to the surface. My body wants to give up, but Guy makes his way to my side. He's much stronger than I am, so it's been easier for him to fight the pull of the current. He takes my hand and points down again. We swim lower.

I wouldn't be able to make it if he wasn't pulling me along with him. Eventually, we come up to the surface for a quick, safe breath of air and go right back down into the water. Since I have Guy to lead me, I close my eyes. I allow my body to go on autopilot and kick wildly behind me while I move wherever Guy wants me to go.

My knee brushes sand, and I pull my body up to a standing position. When I open my eyes, I see that Guy is doing the same. He lets go of my hand, and a wave crashes over me. It's smaller now that we are closer to the shore, so it only throws me toward my end destination. I don't mind the help. I'm struggling, and my legs are so tired; standing on them isn't as thrilling as it should be after what we've just experienced.

Guy begins running through the wading water with his head cocked back and mouth opened toward the sky, drinking in the rain. He let me drink most of the water, so I can imagine he's much more dehydrated than I feel. I try to run as well, but I fall to my knees and desperately crawl to get myself all the way out of the angry sea.

When the wet sand turns from smooth to slightly rough, I know I've made it. I let my body crash onto the shore. I'm not surrounded by water anymore. I've escaped. Only the rain is keeping me wet. I'll take it. I'm on land. Finally.

The feeling is overwhelming. I start to cry, and I cradle my purse against my chest. I'm overjoyed with relief and a new sense of hope, but I'm also mixed with grief and conflicting emotions. I don't know if I should be happy or still terrified of where I am.

*I'm not home. I'm nowhere.*

Sand bunches up around my head. Guy's feet step in front of me. He bends down and grabs me in his arms while I stay curled up in the fetal position. His chest and heartbeat against my ear bring warmth through my body.

I couldn't have gotten through that without him. He saved me and guided me when I didn't think I had any strength left. I owe him my life.

My eyes open when the rain stops falling on my face. We're shaded under a cluster of trees with large, wide leaves. Guy gently sets me down on my feet, and I stand up on my own.

I'm about to open my mouth and say, *Thank you for saving me*, when …

"What the fuck is wrong with you?" Guy shouts at me. "Are you trying to kill us both—again?"

His chest heaves, and I can't tell if it's from exhaustion or anger.

"What are you talking about?" I yell back.

"Why the hell would you take that with you?" He points an accusing finger toward my purse.

Instinctively, I guard it. "I-I-I don't know. I didn't mean to, but I grabbed it, and I just didn't think to take it off." My whining voice begs him to let it go.

"As if we didn't have enough working against us, you had to go and bring your useless purse to a deserted island. Are you fucking crazy?" He paces with ire fuming out of him. "Give me that."

"No!" I scream, tucking my purse in and shielding it from him further. I take a step back as he tries to grab me. "No!"

Guy took my cell phone. I won't let him take my purse.

"What difference does it make?" His frustration with me is palpable.

I've got no defense, and I wish I didn't have to defend myself to him. If he didn't just save my life—*again*—I wouldn't even try.

"It just does."

"Why the hell do you think you need it? It held you back in the water. You could have died," he fumes.

My fingers clench into the leather. Our shouting is barely audible over the downpour of rain.

"Because I'm lost!" I scream, but my voice begins to tremble. Saying those words out loud makes the reality hit me harder than a ton of bricks. I wave my purse up with one hand and shakily hold it up in the air. "This is all I have. If I lose this, I'll have nothing. I'll really have nothing. I know it can't help us, but it's *something*. It's something from where I belong." I look around at this foreign environment. "I don't belong here!" I yell at him.

Tears pour out of me, but I'm too overwrought with grief to make a sobbing sound. I just turn in a circle, taking in our newfound home, and scream to no one but myself, "Ahhh!"

I'm about to take my temper tantrum up a level, but Guy's arms wrap around me from behind. He's not soothing me; his arms are meant to be a cage. He doesn't say a word. He just holds me still, keeping me from further melting into a breakdown and preventing me from going completely insane.

The back of my wet shirt presses against his chest, his pecs padding me. His muscles, confining me, don't twitch or move when I struggle to get free of him. He holds me firm and without remorse. And, eventually, like he wanted, I give up. His strong, tense jaw relaxes and rests on top of my head. Our breathing syncs together, and we meld into each other without a fight. He still doesn't let me go. We sink down to the dirt, still attached to each other. We don't move or talk.

*The apartment is hazy, but the feeling is real. It's a lazy morning, Saturday or Sunday, and we decide to stay in bed. I can see the rays in the room dancing in the air like pixie dust.*

*"What do you want to do today, my dear?" Charles asks with a low, sleepy moan.*

*"Just this," I tell him, savoring the soft feel of the comforter wrapped around me. "I only want to do this."*

*I move, adjusting myself on the bed that I share with my husband in this New York apartment, but I can't get comfortable. He seems to fade away, and the rays consume the room to the point that everything disappears, except one blinding light.*

The harsh realization hits me hard when I open my eyes. I'm faced with the reality that I'm in the dirt and sand with Guy, who is still barely more than a stranger to me. If it wasn't for a plane crash, I'd have only known him as an asshole I met on a plane once.

My clothes are dry, but my back is still against the padding of Guy's chest. His body hair is untrimmed and perking up like a masculine, wild mane. For a moment, I pretend I'm waking up, wrapped in Charles's arms, wishing I could make my dream real. They're the same height, and our bodies spoon together in a similar way, but Charles is softer—his chest hairs, his body. The familiarity is gone, but I can strive and pretend.

Although I'm lying on rough, uneven ground, I try to settle my breathing to sync with Guy's while he's holding me from behind. I embrace his muscles clutching around me. I adjust my backside further into him, finding little comfort on the other side of a tree root that's protruding the ground between us. As I move, my body makes him stir. He inhales deeply at the back of my head and squeezes me tighter into him. I try to close my eyes and return to my dream, but I feel him growing against my lower back.

*Oh shit.*

His pants, worn from being wet, are becoming tattered. The loosened fabric gives it all away. His erection grows until his hardness feels like a solid girth. He's pressing into me. And there it is—that uneasiness in my stomach.

I dash up and scoot myself away from him, facing him on my knees against a nearby bush.

Guy startles awake and moves to an upright position. "What's wrong? What happened?"

I hesitate and scroll my mind for answers. I don't want to tell him I felt him get hard against me. I don't want to address it at all. Not that I care about embarrassing him. I just don't want him to get confused about us being stuck here together. I tuck my lower lip under and bite off a tiny piece of skin that's beginning to chap.

"Um, I thought I saw a spider," I finally say, unsure of my excuse.

He stands up and brushes the dirt off his chest and left shoulder, where he was lying on the ground. "A fucking spider. I have a feeling you're gonna have to get"—his hands continue to brush further down to the left side of his pants, and my eyes nervously watch him—"used to it," he says slowly and hesitantly as he begins to notice I'm staring at his enlarged groin area.

I feel the heat rise in my cheeks, and I hope he doesn't feel too embarrassed. I'm embarrassed for him. Quickly, I look away at something else and then draw my attention back up to his face.

*We can handle this like adults and just pretend it isn't happening.*

A slow and devious grin slides across one side of his mouth. "You might have to get used to a few things around here."

*He's enjoying this?*

I can't feel anything but discomfort. It makes me so uneasy; my neck feels warm, and my chest feels like it's full of lead.

I wish I could expel this awkward and horrible feeling I have.

I want to slap him again. Maybe it would shake some sense and manners into him.

"Uh, pig!" I stand up and start to walk away, but he grabs my arm.

"It's natural. Don't be a prude," he says, losing the humor he had in his voice moments ago. "What do you expect when I wake up with a woman's ass pressed into me?"

I yank my arm free. "I'm not a prude. I just don't want you to get the wrong idea. We're both married."

His lips purse, and he doesn't try to fight me walking away from him anymore.

The rain has stopped, and the sun is becoming brighter as it rises more each minute, spraying the sky with orange and magenta lights mingling with each other. It's beautiful, but I don't care. I make my way down to the now-calm shore and continue to walk away from Guy. I just need a little space to cool off. *He* needs to cool off.

I look back, and he's standing where I left him. His hands on his hips, he watches me.

"We need to find food and make some sort of shelter," he calls out with his hands cupped around his mouth.

*Why couldn't he have just pretended it never happened from the beginning?*

I'm grateful for the distraction now, but it only makes me upset in a different way. I'm reminded we're still lost. This infuriates me further.

"We *need* to get the hell out of here!" I scream in front of me, mostly for my benefit.

Settling in here on this island with Guy is the last thing I want. I want to be rescued.

# *Nine*

I'm not sure how long I've been gone. I can only guess it's been a few hours. Time has much less meaning to me now that there is no clock or schedule to live by. It's only been about four days—*or is it five?*—since we crashed, but it feels like a lifetime. At the very least, I know it's been too long.

In the past few hours, I've gone for a walk around the entire island. It's given me time to cool off and realize that Guy has saved me and helped me too many times for me to hate him over a boner. Although I will do everything in my power to make sure that doesn't happen again. I'll have to try to sleep as far from him as possible while still being safely within his reach in case something terrible happens again.

The sun is out and in full effect.

Guy looks up as I near, using his hand to shade his eyes from the sun at my back. His other hand has a large stick in it. "Hungry?" he asks.

I start to run the rest of the way to him. "You found food?" I ask with desperation.

I could be dreaming about going home to Charles's and my four-thousand-square-foot apartment in Manhattan, but my expectations have dwindled. Now, the best thing that could happen to me is, I would get to eat food and drink water. One out of the two seems very hopeful right now, and it makes me eager to find out what Guy could have possibly found. It could be edible mud for all I care.

Guy turns to his side furthest from me and grabs a three-foot bunch of bananas. He sets them down in front of me as I reach him.

I shake and scream with excitement, "We get to eat!"

"We slept under a banana tree last night," he confirms and points up to the large sprawling leaves above us.

I smile while I hastily grab one and tear it apart from its friends. I'm devouring this banana with my eyes as I peel back the thick yellow skin before shoving the creamy girth of the fruit into my mouth. After the whole banana, I'm still famished. I grab another and just as eagerly pull back the peel.

I shove the next one in my mouth.

*Food … is this heaven?* I never knew how much I would miss it until it was taken away from me.

My eyes roll back in my head as I try to savor this delightful feeling of being fed. It's the same sensation as gasping for air after nearly drowning. It hurts to let go or stop.

I look up to Guy as I take another deep bite. My teeth barely scrape down the sides of the soft banana until I feel like I've gone as deep as I can handle, and I bite into it. His eyes look as hungry as I feel, but I've learned what that look in his eyes means. I've been trying to get over it, but there's no denying it. He's a pig. I know exactly what he's thinking.

"Oh, shut up," I say with my mouth full.

I'm too satiated to care about his grotesque mind. He can keep whatever hard-on he might have to himself. I'm too busy filling myself with food.

Guy reaches down and adjusts himself under his pants. Then, he kneels down to my eye-level. "I think I've just found a new inspiration to survive on this island. If I'd known you liked bananas so much—"

"I don't," I quickly interrupt. "I actually hate bananas," I say as I take another huge bite.

His surprised eyes are laced with humor, which I'm eager to express myself. We begin to laugh as I finish my second banana and grab another.

Guy's gentle hand reaches mine as I touch the next one. "Try to slow down with this one. I don't want you to hurt yourself." Although I know he means it, his words barely come out between his chuckles.

I agree; I should slow down and start pacing myself, but we both begin laughing again. This is the best feeling I've had since I stepped onto the plane. I even find beauty in Guy's smile. I can actually find humor in his nasty thoughts and comments.

I can't help but smirk when I ask, "So, you never told me what you do. How did you get all that money that Marina wants so badly?"

"Well, it wasn't easy," he says, raising his eyebrows and chewing. "I wasn't born with a silver spoon in my mouth."

"Could have fooled me," I tease.

"No. Quite the opposite." He becomes more serious. "My brother and I were raised by a single mother. We all struggled. But I managed to pay my way through a private high school because I knew I couldn't get into Harvard without it. And then I found a way to pay my way through Harvard Business School. And, now, I'm a businessman."

"A businessman? That's very vague. What kind of business?"

"I buy large companies that aren't turning a profit and fix them. I find the right people to make them successful and then sell them for a profit. Not too different from what you do."

"And how do you figure that?" I scoff.

"Oh, I'm sorry, Mrs. Devereux. Have I offended you because you're not the most charitable person in the room?"

"I run a nonprofit. You make money. How does that help anyone but yourself?" I roll my eyes.

"Because I save hundreds of thousands of people from losing their jobs. Saving companies means I'm saving people's income. Income *they* get to keep and use to raise families."

I smile lightly, thinking about the chivalry he sees in his job. "It's still no nonprofit," I try to tease.

"You've got me there," he says, keeping his eyes on me a little too long.

At night, we lie side by side a few yards up from the high tide. I might be fighting my distaste of Guy, but I do love that we can be around each other without the need to talk. Awkward silences aren't so awkward.

We made some headway today on building some kind of shelter. For now, it's just a pallet of wood Guy managed to pull together from fallen branches. We chose the most even ones to make as flat of a surface as possible. It sits below a large banana tree leaf, not far from where we slept last night.

Guy seems to think we can add to the one large leaf and create some sort of roof. It'll do for now, and the pallet will be fine for tonight while the air is calm and an even temperature.

He made the mistake of asking me to remove my engagement ring. He wanted to use it to cut some of the vines into strips that he could braid into rope. I told him he would have to find another way because I had no intention of ever taking my ring off on this island. It stays on because it's the only feeling I have that Charles is with me.

My skin chills slightly as a slow wind passes by. It is a perfect, refreshing breeze, heightened by the beauty of the starry sky. No clouds, no interruptions between my eyes and space.

"I like looking at the stars here."

Guy only subtly nods once. "Better than the raft."

I agree. "Same sky, but it's easier to appreciate from land." I close my eyes and try to imagine looking up to the sky from the middle of Central Park. It's never looked like this before. I open my eyes, and I'm right back where I was. "I just wish we could see it from the city."

Guy nods again. "Some people want what they can't have." He turns his head to look at me. "You can't have this in Manhattan, so instead of wishing you could change it or have both, you need to decide which one you want more."

I turn on my side to look at him before I answer, "Manhattan. No question."

He smiles softly. "Yeah. I might have taken some things for granted, too, but I'd rather be there and have my old problems than the ones we're facing now."

"Thank you," I sincerely say to him, hoping he'll look my way.

He does. "For what?"

Now that I can look him in the eyes, I feel like I can do this the right way. "Thank you for saving my life. Thank you for caring about keeping me alive. I wouldn't have been able to last an hour without you."

His expression deadpans at first until I notice the vulnerability in his eyes.

"You're welcome," he finally answers. "But you're stronger than you think."

"No, I'm not. I'm scared and incapable."

"You're wrong. You've got some fight in you. I can see a feisty woman deep down in there." He gives me a look that reminds me of how uncomfortable he can make me feel.

"Feisty?" I pretend to be insulted. "Don't call me names just because I got mad at your erection the other morning."

Guy laughs. "First of all, feisty is not calling you names. I believe the word I used that morning is prude. But the funny thing is, I don't even think you're prude. I just think you act like it."

"What's the difference?" I entertain this conversation.

"Difference is, you're fooling yourself. Second of all," he goes on to say, "why the hell do you call it an erection? It sounds like you're teaching a sex-ed class."

"Uh," I scoff, "what else would you call it? That's exactly what it was."

Guy rolls onto his stomach. "Try cock and dick. You'll sound more like an adult."

"Co—" I stop myself by putting my hand over my mouth. "I can't say those words."

"Oh, Naomi, who the hell is going to hear you out here? You can scream them if you want to. That's the silver lining of being stranded on an island. Nobody can hear your dirty mouth."

*Cock. Dick.* I try those words in my mind first. They make me want to giggle like a little girl.

"Cock," I say out loud and turn to Guy. "Happy now?"

He seems unimpressed. "Louder, Nay."

"Cock!" I scream and immediately start to laugh.

Guy chuckles, too. "Dick," he encourages.

"Dick!" I yell so loudly that there's an echo around us.

"Pussy." Guy continues to laugh.

"Pussy!"

"Cunt," he tells me to say next.

I gasp. "I can't use that wo—"

There's a crackling sound behind us, and it startles me to look in the direction of the noise. The air becomes still around us, and the mood completely changes.

"What was that?" My eyes search around for any sign of movement.

Guy looks in the same direction, but he doesn't hold the same concerns that I do. "Maybe you're a little bit of a scaredy-cat. It was just a branch falling or a coconut or something. Nothing to worry about."

"You don't think it could have been an animal?" I ask, still wary of what might be out there.

"No," Guy says, rolling onto his back and placing his hands, fingers interlocked, on his chest. "I don't think there are any animals here. I didn't see any signs of animals today. No tracks, no shit, nothing." He turns his head to look at me. "Did you?"

"No, but there might be more to the island than what either of us has seen today." I crane my head to look up to the small mountain that protrudes out of the ocean, creating this piece of land for us. "Maybe there's some five-star resort at the top. Or better, maybe there's a cell tower. At least you still have *your* phone."

I can almost feel Guy's eyes roll.

"Sure, I can go get it at the bottom of the ocean." He stands and holds out his hand for me.

I reach up and let him help me to my feet.

"We can go explore the island more tomorrow. For now, let's try out our new bed."

*Our new bed?*

That sounds so wrong, but there is nothing I can do about it. The only person I should be sharing a bed with is my husband, and he's not here.

We take a few steps in the same direction when Guy says, "Don't worry; I'll sleep with my back to you tonight."

It is as if he was reading my thoughts.

"I think that's a good idea," I agree, but there is a small part of me that will miss the warmth of his body during the night.

This might not be my home—Guy is not home to me—but there is some comfort here even if it's a little. I can hold on to that, can't I?

# Ten

The sun tickles my face with light. I open my eyes with heavy lids, creating a haze of fuzziness in front of me. I blink a few times and allow my eyes to get used to the light. I can't believe I actually had a peaceful night's sleep.

I stretch my arms out and test the limits of my muscles. My body shakes when I push myself to stretch just a little further. It feels good. I move my arm behind me, knowing that nothing is there but I want to check anyway. Nothing.

Rolling over to my other side, I see for myself that Guy is gone.

I get myself up and walk around to stretch my legs. I wonder where Guy went, but it doesn't bother me to be alone. It actually feels kinda nice to have some headspace while he isn't getting on my nerves or killing me with kindness. It feels like a mind game, and I'm mentally exhausted from it.

The banana tree we've been sleeping under, the one with the leaves providing us with the little shelter we have, looks as if it has several thin trunks sprouting out of the ground. They're all in a cluster, making one tree. Just behind it is a rock with a flat top I've been using as a calendar. I bend down and pick up one of the sharp stones Guy used to shape and carve our pallet.

I hate the sound of the two hard rocks sliding against each other. The dry, screeching sound is more bearable than nails on a chalkboard, but it still irks my ears.

*One. Two. Three. Four. Five.*

Yesterday, Guy confirmed it was our fourth day on the island. We were at sea for three days prior, so we've been missing for over a week.

Each day has been getting better, especially after we managed to break open coconuts for the milk. Still, it's not water, and a banana and coconut diet isn't going to be enough to keep us healthy forever. I'd kill to eat a real meal. Perhaps there is something else in this place that can give us more food—or better, fresh water. During the past couple of days, we explored the perimeter of the island, but we have yet to go up the large hill trying to be a mountain on this desolate island.

I sit back on my heels and admire my new daily hobby. I can keep track of how long we're here until someone comes to find us.

The sun behind me becomes shaded, and I know a figure is blocking the light.

"There's something I need to show you." Guy's voice prompts me to stand up and turn to meet his eyes.

"What is it?" Dreams of a five-star resort in the middle of the small island fly into my mind. Yesterday, I was only joking about there being a resort here, but when you feel as desperate as I do, anything seems like a possibility. I'd settle for a porta potty and be really excited about it.

A light smile spreads across his face and lights up his gray eyes. His hand reaches out for me to hold. "It's not something I can describe. I want to show you."

I return his smile and place my hand in his. I like waking up to this version of Guy. Being alone was nice for a few moments, but right now, being with him feels better.

He leads me through flimsy branches and bushes. The uneven terrain hurts my feet, but I've been getting used to it.

"I'll try to cut through here to make an easier path for us."

Reality has set in, and I know for certain there isn't some sanctuary of a resort behind all this foliage, but I'm still excited for what he wants to show me. My anticipation grows with each step.

We reach what looks like a dead end at a bright, vibrant green wall.

"Close your eyes," Guy instructs.

Before I do, I look into his softened dark gray eyes. His quiet, jovial mood is infectious. My mouth curves up, and for a moment, I feel grateful that I'm stuck here with him.

I close my eyes and let him guide me again. When I did this before, it was in desperation and dire need to survive. But, right now, I'm doing it because I trust him, and he asked.

I can hear the branches snapping back and the sound of the fern-like leaves brushing against his arm as he holds them away from my face. He leads me through them until I don't feel anything grazing against me.

My toes sink into soft, muddy ground. I take cautious steps, still holding my eyes closed, and feel thin roots under my feet when the mud squishes between my toes.

Guy's hand holds firm, prompting me to stop. "Okay, open them," he says.

Light fills my eyes with shades of bright baby blue. My mouth drops open, as I'm shocked by all the beauty I see. "Wow," is all I can muster to say.

Guy allows me to gawk and soak it all in. I'm dazzled by the water falling as a white stream from several large boulders hovering over a pool of vibrant blue water below. It's the color of the ocean but surrounded by tropical forest and rocks.

"Where is this water coming from?" I turn to ask Guy.

He shrugs, seeming clueless. "I don't know. I don't get it. There's a pond above the rocks up there." He points to the ten-foot-tall waterfall and shrugs again. "It must somehow be coming from under the ground, or maybe the island is drawing it in from the other side."

I reach my foot out and toe the eighty-degree bath water. "Is it safe to drink?"

Guy furrows his brows in a thoughtful grimace. "I don't think so." He turns to me and grins. "But it's safe to swim in." He reaches over and holds my hand once again.

We start to take a running start through the wading water when I stop. "Wait. We can't go in with our clothes on."

Guy reaches down and pulls his pants to his knees before stepping each leg out and tossing them to dry land. It was way too easy for him to remove his pants without unbuttoning them. He's lost some weight. I have, too. My skirt is barely holding on to my hip bones.

"Way ahead of you." He stands proudly in his boxers.

I think about reaching down to my blouse buttons and doing the same, but I hesitate. It's one thing to do things to ensure our survival, but I can't betray Charles like this—by choosing to be naked with another man. I just can't.

"Look," I begin to speak, removing Guy's smile from his face and replacing it with his full concentration, "I'm married. We're both married. I can't take my clothes off in front of you."

Guy throws his head back and scoffs. "Who the hell is going to know? I'm practically divorced. I don't care if you're married. I just want to live, and if jumping into a pool of water with you can bring me any kind of joy in this hellhole, then I'm going to do it."

"You're not actually divorced. What would your wife—" I begin to reason with him before he jumps in to interrupt me.

"Fuck her," he spits out.

I take a step back. "Well, that's not how I feel about my husband. I have a lot more respect for him than that."

Guy grabs my hand. "Well, where is he then?"

He jabs his finger into his chest, pointing at his unkempt mane. The stubble on his face is beginning to match the unruly nature of his chest hairs. I've never seen a man so masculine. I swallow hard, waiting for his next words.

"I'm the one here with you. After everything we've been through, I deserve some respect, too."

I sharply breathe in, gathering my strength once again to argue with him. I feel so uncomfortable in my gut right now. I feel the urge to fight him. "Just because you've helped keep me alive and I'm stuck here on this island with you doesn't mean I'm going to have sex with you."

Guy blinks with a tiny wave of shock before looking me up and down. I feel as if I should cover myself. I see his Adam's apple bob as he pushes some gathered saliva down his throat.

"Don't be such a snob, Naomi." He steps to walk past me, but as he passes, he says, "Believe me, if I had tried to have sex with you, you wouldn't be so obviously sexually frustrated." His voice lowers to a raspy, virile whisper at the side of my ear. "You would have been begging me for more before I was even done." He keeps walking away from me, and with my back to him, I hear him yell, "You take the first swim. I'll try to go figure out how to get us out of this fucking place."

He disappears behind the foliage with angry swats at the branches in his way. I feel a tingling pulse between my legs as his words echo back into my mind. It was more than what he said; it was his voice and the way he said it. I shake my head, trying to rid myself of these thoughts.

Once the crackling leaves and the sound of branches breaking fade into the distance, I start unbuttoning my shirt. I strip down until I'm completely naked. It's been a while since I've felt air over the entire surface of my skin. We've been sleeping in our clothes for days. I bend over to step out of my panties and place them on the pile with the rest of my ragged outfit.

Once I walk far enough into the water for it to cover my body, I allow myself to float. If I close my eyes, I can pretend I'm in a bath in our Upper East Side apartment. Trees could be the skyline shading the sun as it passes each building throughout the day.

My fingers run over my rib cage and bump up as I move them over each rib. Then, I lay the flat of my palm on my stomach. I can feel my heartbeat in my middle. *Yes, it's mine.* I've given up hope that I could have someone growing inside me. At this point, it's probably a blessing. I'm trying to hold on, but every day, I lose hope of being rescued. Hope seems to work in dog years when you're desperate, alone, and stranded. But I'm not alone.

My hand travels further down and hovers over my coarse hairs. I'm growing a wild mane of my own. I've always kept myself clean and shaven—Charles preferred it—but there's nothing I can do about my hygiene or appearance now.

Guy was out of line, pretending as if I was imagining that he wanted me. As if I was being self-centered. I can tell. I give him a hard-on every time I bend over to pick something up. Sometimes, when I talk to him, he's staring at my lips, not my eyes. They might be in close proximity, but I can see the hunger inside of him.

This tension we feel is only because of him.

Men, by nature, are more sexual creatures than women. I always felt like I was lucky because Charles and I seemed to be on the same page. Sex had a purpose for us, and it wasn't our pastime, like some men want to make it out to be. I'm glad Charles wasn't always pining at me to spread my legs. How exhausting.

Look at me, thinking about Charles as if our life together is in the past.

*Oh God, what if it is?*

# Eleven

My eyes close, and I continue to drift in the peaceful water, listening to the serene sounds of the waterfall in the far corner behind me. My hand is still lying on top of my pubic hairs as I weave my fingers through them, attempting to comb out the coarseness.

My fingertip brushes my clit, and my stomach tenses. I've never touched myself like this before. I can't explain why I feel the need to. Nobody is around, but I stand up and put my feet on the ground at the bottom of the pool so that I can look around, just in case. Nobody in the world. Nobody for hundreds of miles—except for Guy, but he left so angry that I'm sure he won't return anytime soon.

Now that I'm standing up, I reach back down and move past my collection of hairs bunched above the slit between my legs.

My chin and thighs quiver when I brush past my clit again. It's such an intense feeling. I instantly crave another touch once the feeling has rippled its way out of my body. I curl my fingers back to touch it again.

I close my eyes and try to imagine being in my husband's arms. Charles's soft body connected to mine. All I can imagine is comfort—soft, easy comfort.

I open my eyes to reset myself before closing them again. This time, I imagine Guy's carnal voice and his hard, muscular body. I think about his rigid form, his abs, and his protruding hip bones where his muscles curve around to make deep pockets before diving into a V-shaped mystery below his sagging slacks.

I rub my fingers around and then up and down. With Guy's voice ringing in my ears and his rough face scratching against my cheek, I imagine him rubbing himself up and down on me. I think of him hard, like I saw him a few mornings ago. I think of him unleashed and on top of me.

I'm inspired to dip my fingers inside my own body. I poke and press, trying to find some additional pleasure. It feels good, but I need so much more. I can't come from penetration anyway, but in my fantasy, I do.

My fingertips come back to my outer skin where I can concentrate on my clit, hidden between my folds.

This is the first time I've done this. I had no idea I could give myself so much pleasure. I continue to dream and touch myself as my mind travels wildly through the idea of Guy being the one touching me. Without his argumentative words, he's silent with only his rugged and manly body pleasing mine.

I allow that same buildup of nerves Guy gives me when he makes me uncomfortable to grow. It grows into a big pile of energy, wanting to detonate.

*Relax*, I tell myself. *Let it go. Let your body have this.*

And it spreads like an oozing, prickling tension, unraveling and traveling through my lower insides. I feel it in my blood, waving through me in aftershocks. With my eyes still closed, I allow it to do its work and take me from a slow descent into ecstasy and back to reality.

When the air and water begin to feel normal around my skin and I'm back in the world as I know it, I open my eyes.

*Oh shit. That was so much better than a vibrator after sex.*

I never knew I could make my body feel so good. I didn't know that level of pleasure existed. And, even better, it's something I can do to myself.

My joy is soon replaced with guilt and thoughts of my husband. *Where did he go in this fantasy, and why did Guy replace him?*

Yes, Guy is mind-blowingly gorgeous, but I don't love him. Not like I love Charles.

Once I get back to what's the beginning structure of our hut, I feel self-conscious around Guy, and I think he can tell. He tries to ignore the awkward tension between us and takes off to bathe in the pool himself. When he comes back from the pool, things seem to go back to normal.

"Just a few more days, and I'll have all the walls up around the pallet. We'll just need a roof after that," Guy says with his back to mine as we lie down to get rest for the night.

I can't stop thinking about this afternoon, our argument, and then after—the way I touched myself, thinking about him. I scoot myself another inch farther away from his backside.

He seems to notice my movement. He turns his head up and twists his shoulders, as if he wants to say something to me. I turn onto my back, so I can listen.

"I'm sorry about earlier today. I didn't intend to make you uncomfortable. I just wanted to show you something I thought might make being here a little better."

I allow his apology to sink in a few moments before forming a response. "I'm sorry, too. I wish I weren't so prude, but I'm just not a sexual person. I'm not very easily comfortable. Especially …" I hesitate, thinking of the right words to say.

Guy tries to hide a smile behind his lips, but I can see them twitching, resisting the urge to fight his grin.

"What?" I ask, feeling nervous about allowing myself to be so honest and vulnerable about sex in front of him.

He shakes away the dimples that creased in his cheeks when he was trying not to smile. "Nothing."

"No, really. What?" Now that it's out there, I have to know what he's thinking, or my imagination will torture me and further my embarrassment.

His head moves back and forth while he stares up above him. "I just can't understand why you think you aren't a sexual person." He turns his head to face me, and his eyes draw up and down my body. "I feel like you want to jump out of your own skin sometimes because you're so charged. Your skin tone changes, your breathing increases, your muscles twitch."

"No," I laugh. "That's me just being uncomfortable."

"Look at you. You're stunning. There's nothing to make you feel uncomfortable. Own your body." His eyes graze me again, and the pit in my stomach fills with uneasiness. "It's perfect," he says softly.

I feel my cheeks fill with blood and heat. I want to cover up, but there is nothing I can do. I'm completely exposed to him with only my clothes to guard me from his prying eyes. I try not to squirm, but my body wants to move.

"How could you say that? You're married to Marina Cary. She is the mold of a perfect body," I say while half-rolling my eyes up.

He looks back up above him and sticks his elbows out, placing his hands under his head. "She's pretty, but she lost my attraction toward her a long time ago. You need more than a pretty face and body."

"Why do you seem so angry with her? If you married her, didn't you love her?"

I can see his chest rise and fall as he thinks. His breathing is deep and slow.

"I told you I married her for the wrong reasons. For me, it was about having a beautiful woman on my arm. I wanted to make the world envious of me. I felt like I had something to prove, and she was a part of it. For her, it was about lifestyle, image, and money. Our arrangement would have worked if ..." His lips tuck under, as if he's hiding something. He bites his lower lip and slowly releases it. "But then we both hurt each other. I've never actually admitted this to anyone, maybe not even myself until now, but it was my fault everything fell apart." He turns his face toward mine and shows me his devious smile. "And I think you know how much of an asshole I can be."

I reach over and touch his arm. "People make mistakes. You're not always an asshole, and when you're not, you're one of my favorite people to be near. Maybe, when we find a way to get home, you can fix your mistakes, and you and Marina can work things out."

"We're not going to work it out, Naomi. Some things can't be fixed because they were never meant to be whole to begin with. I hate it because I know it's my fault, but I don't blame her for cheating. I just hate who she did it with. I've been punishing her for so long; it's time we both move on."

"No." I shake my head. "I can't believe that. A marriage can always be worked on. Sometimes, you have to suck it up, Guy." My tone is gentle while I place my hand on his forearm.

He reaches over to my hand on his arm and lifts it up. I think he's going to try to hold my hand, but instead, he places it away from him and puts it back on my own body.

"Like I've said before, people cheat. Mine was bad, hers was worse, and then neither of us stopped."

I'm glad I'm not touching him anymore because, if I were, I'd be digging my nails into his skin. "You cheated on her first?" I ask with disgust.

"But then she slept with my brother," he quickly retorts, indirectly answering my question.

I put my hands in the air with defeat. His marriage is, or was, more fucked up than I could have imagined.

"I'm not a marriage counselor. You're right; maybe it's a good thing for you two to get divorced. But you're wrong about people—at least other people. *We* don't cheat."

I'm talking to myself much more than Guy. I don't cheat. I'd like to believe that other people don't cheat, too, but Guy has proven that wrong, and I know how naive I am to think he and his wife are the only ones.

*I don't cheat.* That's all that matters. But I can't for the life of me figure out why I feel the need to keep reminding myself.

"Let's just not talk about this anymore," Guy says.

"I think that's a good idea."

He rolls back, facing away from me. "I think we should try to get up as high as we can on the island tomorrow to get a better vantage point. That way, we can see if anything is out there in the distance."

"Fine," I agree, but my mind is still brewing and upset over our previous conversation.

# Twelve

We pass by the pool that forms after the small waterfall. I think about what I did to myself in there yesterday, but then I stop, realizing I don't have room for the kinds of thoughts with Guy in them … or with him around.

Behind the waterfall is another pool of water; rocks and boulders outline the ponds, giving it a man-made feel—nature at its best.

"Let's try to take this path on the side here." He points to my left. "It looks like the easiest way up."

Guy holds his hand out for me to use him as leverage as I jump from one large rock to another. I follow him, focusing on my feet and where my next step will be. It's not terribly high up, but it's steep.

"This is my first time hiking."

Guy places his hand on a large rock to his side, giving him leverage to scoot up to a higher rock. Once he's there, he turns and offers his hand to me.

"See?" he says. "You have an adventurous side after all."

I smile at the thought. He's right. I love how the view seems to change with every step. I'm probably exploring territory that nobody else has ever explored before. Just Guy and me.

"So, what would you call this? A very big hill or a tiny mountain?" I ask between steps.

"For all we know, it could be a volcano," he answers while breathing hard. He's not just trekking uphill on his own; he's also holding and guiding me along the way. "Let's just call it a mountain for shits and giggles."

I laugh out loud. "Shits and giggles, huh?"

Guy stops to smile at me. "What? You don't like my phrases?"

Shaking my head, I say, "Mr. Harrington, you definitely have a way with words. One way or another, you always seem to get a reaction out of me."

He turns to continue climbing up our little mountain. "Mr. Harrington is too formal. I only allow people to call me Guy." He takes one long stride up a boulder and turns to reach his hand out for me. "Especially you."

"Why especially me?" I ask, taking his hand and letting him easily hoist me up to his level.

"Because, as far as I'm concerned, you're the only woman in the world."

The rock we're standing on together doesn't have too much surface area on top. We're inches from each other. His arms are wrapped around me, keeping me from falling off this small space. Our noses are almost touching, and the heat from our breaths is mingling every time we breathe out.

There's nowhere else to look, except into each other's eyes. I feel him wanting to be even closer. It would be so easy to give in, but I hold myself back.

"But you know that's not true," I say only an inch from his mouth, instantly cutting the tension between us.

He lets me go with one arm and reaches up to cup his fingers around a rock's ledge.

"Here, scoot to the side of me, and I'll push you up to the next rock. I don't think we have too much more to climb. I think it gets flat at the top."

I do what he said, moving on from that intense moment. I'm feeling proud of myself. The more I'm around Guy, the easier it feels to fall into his temptation. It's confusing, being here with him for so long and not knowing when we'll ever be rescued … or if we'll ever be rescued. But I'm faithful to Charles, and nothing—not all the time in the world, not the most pristine, masculine man—can shake that.

There are a few more difficult maneuvers, but we make it to the crest of the mountain. It's maybe about five hundred feet of flat surface. Larger than I would have thought. We feel a lot higher up than I would have thought, too.

"Doesn't look like a volcano," I observe.

Guy nods. "I guess it will be our mountain then."

*Our mountain?* I can't encourage that *or* deny his wording. We are the only ones here.

We look out to the expansive sky. Only a few wispy clouds are in the distance. We turn in a circle, taking in the atmosphere from every angle.

"It's beautiful up here," I say into the gentle wind.

I feel Guy's eyes on me, but I don't acknowledge him. I can't lie to myself and say that I don't like his growing affection and doting on me. I'm growing more and more dependent on it. But I can't give into it. I keep my eyes straight ahead.

For some reason, my arm isn't getting the message. I move my fingers out toward his until I feel the back of his hand. His fingers twitch once he feels my touch, and we subtly hook our fingers into each other.

Guy exhales suddenly and harshly. "Look, over there."

He releases my hand, and I look to where he's pointing, to the side of me and off into the far distance.

I start waving my arms up in the air, making huge Xs and shouting, "Hey! Hey! Over here!"

Guy grabs my arms and pulls them down. "Save your breath. They are too far away to see us, let alone hear you."

Against my instincts, I hold still, and Guy and I watch the faraway airplane go from a small jet in the distance to a little blip in the air to nothing.

My nose gets warm, and I scrunch it up, trying to hold back the tears that are beginning to form. Guy sees my struggle, so he brings me into his body and wraps his arms around me.

"We're never getting out of here, are we?" I sob into his neck.

His hand moves up and caresses my hair. "I don't know, but I promise, we'll be okay. I won't let anything happen to you."

I sniffle and lean back to look at him. "The only reason I'm alive is because of you." I lick my lips before allowing myself to go further and be completely honest with him. "The only reason I want to be alive is because you're here with me."

He breathes in and brushes my hair out of my eyes. I turn my face away from him so as not to give him the wrong idea. I feel like I need to be near him and hold on to him, but I don't want to let things go where they cannot.

Guy takes my hint and only pulls me in for another hug. This time, I have dry eyes. We stand there, on top of our mountain, for a few minutes, just embracing each other.

"We should head back down. It looks like there are some rain clouds in the distance. If they come this way, it'll take a few hours to reach us. We need to get ready to collect as much rainwater as we can."

I nod. "Okay."

He lets me go, and I take a few steps but stumble over a rock on the ground. I fall on the dirt and roll over on my back, giving in to my clumsiness.

Guy kneels down beside me. "Graceful." He laughs.

I laugh at myself, too. He reaches down to grab under my arm to help me up but stops. He moves his face closer to mine. Again, I'm growing more comfortable with the familiarity of him being close to me. His hand moves over to my face, and his warm palm feels so good on my cheek.

He smiles. "You've got a little dirt on your face."

His hand goes from my cheek up to my forehead, and he places the pad of his thumb on my temple and wipes across.

Immediately, I feel guilty and out of place.

I abruptly sit up and move to my feet. "I think we should go."

I don't wait for Guy's reaction. I just begin walking, finding the path we took to get up here.

He follows behind and calls out to me, "What just happened? Did I do something wrong? I felt like you—"

"No. We just need to go. Let's just go, so we're ready for the rain," I say, continuing to walk, not turning back toward him.

We don't speak as we carefully descend. Guy is just as strong and protective of me through the terrain as he was going up. But the mood between us has changed.

After we pass the two pools and waterfall and go through the still-overgrown foliage, we make it back to our almost complete hut. The sky dims but no rain yet.

Guy finally speaks to me, "What is it with the mood swings?"

I turn and face him, jabbing my finger into my chest. "Me? You invented mood swings!" I yell back to him.

He catches my arm and opens his mouth to say something else, but I yank myself away from him.

"This is not what you think!" I yell at him, knowing he has the wrong idea about what's happening between us.

"This is exactly what I think, and you know it. You know it because you wouldn't be reacting this way if it wasn't!" he yells at me just as loudly as I was yelling at him.

I reach up, put my fingers into my hair, and pull. "I can't stand you!"

"Yes, you can. And you'd better because I'm all you've got," he says, defending himself with his hands on his hips, exposing his chest and ab muscles even more.

I notice them, and I breathe in heavily. It frustrates me even more. "You are not all I've got." A lone sprinkle of rain falls on my cheek. "I have Charles. And just because we haven't been found *yet*"—I emphasize *yet* with everything I have in me—"doesn't mean you're not still married. You might be an adulterer, but I'm not."

I turn my back to him and attempt to flee farther away from him. I've said my piece, and now, I want to stew in my anger.

He grabs me by both arms and spins me around to face him, as if I have no control over it. "We might never leave this island. We might *never* be found."

"No," I say unconvincingly.

Another drop of rain falls on my arm and then another. Several begin to fall between Guy and me. He's unfazed at first, still gripping my arms as if his life depended on it, until the rain becomes so constant that it's impossible to ignore.

He lets go. His dark gray eyes brighten as he says, "Water. Let's get the cups."

A few days ago, Guy made several cups and bowls out of some of the banana leaves that had fallen on the ground.

We both run behind the hut where the cups are lined up, ready for the rain. We each grab two and hold them up in the air, capturing as much drinkable water as possible.

The rain continues to pour down and fully wets my clothes and body. It's a welcome, impromptu shower. Once one of my cups fills up about halfway, I drink. The delight of having water—fresh water moving down me and hydrating my insides—makes me smile. Not just any smile, but a beam, as if brightness came out of my soul. I'm so happy just to have a little bit of water.

I dance and drink and laugh in the rain. Guy is doing the same. He's running around as if he just hit a home run, yelling and laughing with me. Our bad moods are gone, and now, we are merely surviving in unison with each other. At the moment, we're enjoying it.

But he's right; we might not ever get off this island. He really is all I have, but I can't let him know that.

# Thirteen

The rain gave us ten cups of water to save. We drank as much as we could during the passing storm, but we don't know when the next one will come. In between rain showers, we'll have to drink the extra cups of fresh water we store, and then we'll survive on coconut milk.

"I'm so sick of bananas," I groan, throwing my peel into the plants behind me.

Guy is standing in front of me, blocking the sun, folding another banana leaf into a cup, preparing for our next storm. "It might be easy enough to trap some fish, but I don't know how to make a fire to cook it."

I stand up on my feet and dust the sand off me. "Can't we just rub a couple of sticks together? Like the Boy Scouts do. You seem like the Boy Scout type to me."

Guy smirks and twists one side of his mouth up. "I'm so glad you find me so impressive. Hey, where are you off to?" he asks as I move away toward the back of the hut.

"I'll be right back. I'm just going to mark another day in the calendar."

I bend over the flat-top rock we began making tally marks on. I cringe at the sound as I force the rock to make a line. I sit back and count the days. I haven't done that for a while. Being on this island is beginning to feel too routine.

I'm one strike away from fifteen days. We've been on this deserted island for two weeks. I stand up and place my hand on my middle. I look down.

*Holy shit. Holy shit. I'm pregnant. I must be pregnant.*

My hand circles around in a slow, soothing motion, but then I stop.

*No. No, I can't be.*

This can't be good, but I don't want to get my hopes up. Even being here, lost and fighting to find new ways to continue our survival every day, I want this. I want to be pregnant, but I don't want to be wrong. Even in the middle of nowhere, the blow would crush me.

It's only been two weeks. Maybe I'll start my period today.

*Wait!*

We were on the raft, floating in the middle of the ocean, for three days. That makes my period days late.

*I'm never late!*

I take a moment and try to think, but my mind only circles around the fact that something is growing inside me. I breathe in deep and imagine Charles putting his arms around me as we find out together. He should be here for this moment. He has wanted this as badly as I have. It isn't fair. Still, I want to be sure, even surer than I feel now.

Coming back around to the entrance of our little hut, I try to act natural. I don't want Guy to know what's going through my mind—or my body. I don't want to think about the consequences and obstacles that might present themselves with a pregnancy this far away from civilization. But I'm a woman. I have instincts, and women had babies long before doctors and hospitals were around.

*I can do this,* I reassure myself once more. *I've survived a plane crash, and I've climbed a mountain. I can have a baby on a deserted island if I have to.*

I crouch down beside my purse, which is tucked in the corner, out of the way from the room we have to sleep in. At least Guy respected my wishes enough not to throw my purse into the ocean. We both knew it didn't serve us any purpose here, but he understood that I needed it as a reminder of what we were trying to get back to. Now, I realize its contents might actually be useful.

It's not a large bag, but I found ways to hide and conceal my personal items. Unzipping the back pocket, I pull out one of three items I know is in there. A tampon.

*I'm not going to need this.*

I set it down beside me and reach in again. My little two-inch travel vibrator. I hold it and smile at the smooth, shiny silver tool.

*You did a good job*, I silently speak to it, thinking about how it must have helped me conceive.

I set it down on the floor beside my tampon.

My stomach churns with nerves and anticipation. It's a long shot, I know, but it might just work. My hand reaches into my inside purse pocket one last time. I pull out a pregnancy test.

The faux plastic package looks as if it's been through as much torment as I have. I pinch the end of it to see if air fills the other end of the wrapping, inspecting it for any holes. My fingers squeeze at the bottom …

"What the hell is that?" Guy's obnoxious tone travels in the hut.

Quickly, I pull the pregnancy test to my side farthest from him and tuck it between the elastic band in my underwear and my hip. I've lost a lot of weight, so my clothes are loose on my body, but the elastic is holding out just enough so that, if I don't make any abrupt movements, it won't fall and expose my vulnerability right now.

I look beside me, where his line of sight is focused. I swallow, gathering the nerve and courage to confront him in a way that will get him out of my face the fastest. "It's a tampon," I say as sarcastically as possible.

Hopefully, if he knows he's not embarrassing me, he'll want to move on.

His stare moves to my side. "I know what a goddamn tampon is. What the fuck is that?"

I can't tell if he's confused or angry.

*Oh shit. Maybe this is embarrassing for me.*

I feel like I want to shrink down even further, but I know I have to appear strong.

"It's nothing. Just mind your own business."

I grab my tampon and vibrator in my fist and stand up. I try to pass him in the threshold to the hut, but he grabs my wrist hanging at my side. I'd rather chance him going for my fist with my personal items in it than bump him on the side carrying the pregnancy stick.

I freeze as soon as he grabs me, not wanting to give my other hip any sudden movements.

"What's your problem?" I calmly say.

"What's yours?" he replies, furrowing his brows, looking perplexed.

He pulls my hand up and pries my fingers open. I don't resist much since I don't want to make a bigger deal out of this than necessary. My fingers lay flat, exposing my vibrator and tampon.

He grabs the tampon and tosses it over his shoulder. "I'm sure that's ruined. I don't think it would be sanitary to put it"—his eyes narrow down to my crotch—"there."

He picks up the vibrator and holds it up closer to his eye-level. He clicks on the small bottom button. Nothing happens. Obviously, it didn't survive a plane crash and washing up on shore. Electronics aren't meant to survive in the water.

Guy looks past the vibrator between his fingers and smiles at me as if I were here for his own personal amusement. "Naomi, come on. Of all things, what the hell was this doing in your purse?"

"None of your business." I move to snatch it out of his hand, but he's too fast.

"Uh-uh. No. You can't get out of this one." He leans back against the hut and crosses his arms. "We've got nothing to do today. Tell me why in the world you carried a tiny vibrator around with you."

I exhale and roll my eyes before I begin to reluctantly explain. Looking away from him, I say, "Because Charles and I are …" I clear my throat and correct myself, "*Were* trying to get pregnant."

Guy shrugs and flips my sex tool up in the air. He catches it and asks with a smirk, "So, what do you need a vibrator for?"

I bite my lower lip. "Because it helps if a woman orgasms."

His eyes narrow, and he stands up with a more erect posture. He takes a step closer toward my face, invading my personal space. "So, what do you need a vibrator for?" he asks again.

My throat suddenly feels dry, so I force a collection of saliva and push it down. "Be-because not everyone can orgasm from penetration. A-a-and it's none of your business," I try to say with confidence.

I place my right hand on my hip, securing the pregnancy test to my hip even tighter, and push Guy out of my face with my other hand. I walk away from him, but he follows me.

"You can't be serious, Naomi." He's not laughing anymore. In fact, he seems angry.

"I am serious that it's none of your business. Now, leave me alone!" I am beyond embarrassed, and I feel violated and defensive. I shouldn't be discussing my vibrator with him. This should be between me and my husband.

He runs his hands up in his hair and grips with frustration. "Come on. What kind of a husband do you have?"

He's visibly upset, and it makes no sense to me.

*It's none of his goddamn business.*

I turn toward him and take a few steps with my finger darting out. "Don't you dare bring him up. He's a better husband than you!" I yell at him with a few tears welling up in my eyes.

Guy is attacking the father of my child, and I'm the only one here to defend him.

Guy stops in his tracks and glares at me. I've hurt his feelings, but I don't care.

After taking a few breaths to calm down, I ask, "What did you think it was for? Weren't you fishing for that answer from the beginning? Now, you have to humiliate me?"

He looks to the side and then back to me. "No, Naomi, I wasn't fishing for that answer. I thought …" His lips twitch for a moment before he continues, "I just thought you wanted it for yourself just in case you were alone somewhere. I didn't think you needed it to be with someone else." His tone is sincere and almost remorseful.

My cheeks flush, and my eyes fill with tears once again. I'm not sure if I want to cry because I miss Charles or because I'm embarrassed, and Guy is the last person I wanted to know about my trouble with orgasms … or lack thereof.

"Naomi." He takes a step toward me and then stops. "Nay, I just feel …" Taking a moment to collect his thoughts, he shakes his head. "I don't know what I feel. Forget it. I'm sorry I pried. Just forget it. I'll leave you alone."

Good. That's what I want, but for some reason, I feel unfinished. I'm surprised he's giving up so soon. I expected him to be more of an asshole. His sudden retreat leaves me feeling unfulfilled.

"Okay then," I say, hesitating, turning to walk away from him. "I'm going to go pee now. I'd like some privacy." My hand falls back down to my hip, and I walk into the foliage, leaving Guy behind so that I can test my fate.

# Fourteen

The plane crash has forced me to do a lot of things I never considered doing. I never thought I could pee outdoors. I can't recall a time I ever tried. But it's something I've gotten used to now.

Before I squat down, I inspect the package wrapped around the stick I'm supposed to pee on.

*Damn, there's a tear.*

I pull at the corner and fully expose the pregnancy test. The plastic cap is cracked, and the foam tip has already been saturated with water. The center of the plastic stick has only one pink line—*negative*. Of course it's negative; the ocean water is the only thing that it tested.

It's useless to me now.

"Fuck," I say out loud and toss the pregnancy test deep into the wall of bright green trees.

All I can do now is wait. Either my belly will start to get bigger or I'll get my period. Until I know for sure, I'll just have to assume I'm pregnant.

I didn't really need to pee, but since I'm here and I have privacy, I'll take the opportunity. I squat down and do my business as I think about what it might be like to have a baby here. It's not just me. Whether he likes it or not, Guy will have to help me.

I dread the idea of telling him. I can only imagine the disappointment he'll feel.

"During which one of your crazy adventures did you learn to make a fire?" I say as I watch Guy rub two sticks on top of a small pile of leaves.

He looks up and smiles as he moves his hands back and forth so fast. It creates a little smoke. "None of them. This is all new to me. But I did have a TV." He looks back down to concentrate on what he's doing. "And," he adds, "I watched a few episodes of *Survivor*."

The sky is getting darker by the minute. The sun went down behind our mountain, and soon, it will be swallowed by the sea on the other side of the island. The past couple of weeks have been warm, even at night, but the past couple of days have been chilly whenever the wind blows through our hut. We've been sleeping closer and closer, inching our way toward each other.

I rub my shoulders up and down with my hands. "Well, I'd pay a lot of money for cameramen to jump out and surprise us and tell us we're actually just on a TV show."

More smoke billows up from the crushed pile of leaves. I kick the sand in front of me.

There is so much more on my mind than Guy realizes. My mind is focused on the life that's likely been created inside me. But I know what a fire would mean; it's more food, a distress signal, and warmth.

"Ah! Ha! Ha-ha-ha-ha! I did it!" Guy yells.

I turn to look at a beautiful little fire. The way the orange, yellow, and auburn movements dance in front of the darkening plush green island behind it, it's a color combination I've never seen before. It's gorgeous.

"You did it!" I scream up into the air.

Guy tends to the growing flames and feeds more dry foliage into the fire. My body takes over, and I begin to jump and dance around. The song "We Didn't Start the Fire" plays in my mind.

*We did. We did start the fire!*

He stands up and joins me, dancing around. "We did it!" he exclaims.

I bounce to face him. "No, you did it!"

He reaches out for my hand, and I place my palm on his. Pulling me in, he says, "I did it for you." We sway with me close in his arms. "You're the only reason I'm surviving, too, Naomi," he whispers into my ear. "I wish I could give you the life you deserve, but this is all we have."

His sweet words seep into my mind. He's right; he is all I have. This island is all I have, and right now, it feels like enough. I'd rather be with Charles, warm and protected inside our Manhattan apartment, but Guy can be enough for me here.

I breathe in and settle my cheek on his growing beard. "We have each other," I reassure him.

Our bodies move closer and closer, and I can feel my middle touching his rippled abs.

*And there might be someone else to take care of, too*, I think to myself.

Without Guy's prompting, I reach my arm up around his neck, drawing closer to him with each breath. I mean to pull back and find his dark gray eyes, but I feel reluctant to bring my face further from his. I don't want to lose the contact I have, but I want to add more depth by looking into his eyes.

I can barely pull away, still touching the side of our noses together. Our lips have only a thin layer of air between them. I breathe in the scent of his lips. It's intoxicating, leaving me dizzy and mindless. This is my limit.

Just as I begin to pull away and push against him, he moves in. For a split second, I feel his lips on mine. The warmth spreads through my mouth and covers my insides. Explosions of tingles linger where we touched, but I ignore it and continue to push away.

"Nay," he begins to say, but I stop him.

"No. No, that was all I had. This can't go any further."

I begin to walk away toward the fire, but my hand remains connected to his. He concedes, but like me, he doesn't let go of my hand. We walk together and stand, staying warm in front of the flames. I silently muse about what just happened—what could have happened between us if I hadn't had the strength to stop it.

My mind is clouded with what-ifs.

*What if we get rescued? I couldn't live with myself for betraying Charles's trust.*

*What if we never get rescued? I could live here with Guy. I could be happy, settling into him and allowing his hands to explore my body.*

But I'm stuck in limbo between those two ideas. My hand reaches over my belly button.

Then, there's this secret I'm keeping that neither of them know about.

The evenings are easier with a fire to warm up to before bed. It's especially satisfying to have new and more fulfilling meals throughout the day. Crab and fish are a refreshing change from the coconut and banana diet we were previously on.

I tried to swim out deeper to see if there were more fish farther out, but Guy told me never to go that far out on my own.

"I've seen a few jellyfish once the ocean bottom drops. We'll have to fish where it's shallower, and we can see through the water. There might be water snakes, too. We have to be able to see what's around us."

"No problem. I won't be going anywhere a snake might sneak up on me. But jellyfish? Come on," I tease. "I thought you were tougher than that."

"I'm tough enough to respect things that might kill us. The ocean, for one. But you're right; most jellyfish can't kill you, but a box jellyfish can, and it wouldn't take much. So, just stay out of the dark water."

"Okay," I agree.

An airplane flew by yesterday, early evening, while we were just building the fire up to a large blaze. It wasn't directly over us, but it was closer than the last one we had seen. We have no idea if anyone saw us or if they would know we were stranded if they did.

My false hope is dwindling by the day, and my life as I know it now feels more and more permanent. I'm coming to terms with it.

Guy and I have a smooth rhythm with each other. It's even been a couple of days since we last had an argument. It was something stupid about how I rolled up my skirt to fit tighter around my waist. I think I'm beginning to understand that he starts fights when he's frustrated. I know how he looks at me. I know what he wants. My skirt being hiked up even higher is one of the things that frustrates him. Once I understood that, I didn't take his comments so seriously. I didn't egg him on or participate in his argument, so it dissipated quickly. So quickly that I found myself falling asleep on his chest moments later—just how I woke up this morning. It's become a comfortable place for me.

I make another mark in the calendar—twenty days.

"Naomi!" Guy screams from afar. "Naomi!"

I can hear his vibrating voice bounce off the island trees. He's not just calling to get my attention. Something is wrong. His scream is more of a howl. I try to track where the sound is coming from and begin walking that way.

"What?" I answer him with the same urgency.

I step through winding branches, scratching my legs on rogue twigs as I push through. Every few seconds, he screams my name again until I see him in the distance, deep in the trees.

He screams at me one more time, holding something up in the air. "Naomi! Where the hell did this come from?"

*Oh fuck.*

# Fifteen

"Guy, don't," I try to yell over his screaming voice. He's going on and on, not making any sense.

"Guy, stop. It's not what you think!" I finally get him to take a breath and listen to me. "Just stop!"

He breathes heavily, waiting for me to explain but I'm at a loss for words. My mind seems to have gone blank. He should have come to the conclusion that I'm not pregnant based on the result, but he obviously hasn't taken the time to think about that. Guy's worst quality is that he acts impulsively—probably what led to him cheating.

"Tell me you're not pregnant. Tell me you haven't hidden this from me," he says after my silence has gone on too long for him to take. "After everything we have been through, tell me you haven't been keeping this from me," he demands impatiently.

I open my mouth to speak, but nothing comes out.

"Tell me you're not pregnant!" he yells.

"I can't," I finally blurt out. "I can't tell you I'm not pregnant because I don't know. Maybe I am, but I don't know. Not really."

He holds the test up closer to my face. "Well, what the hell does this mean? Are you, or aren't you?"

I swipe it out of his hand, and he surprisingly lets me. When we've argued in the past, he has always fought to control everything he can.

"The package was ripped, and the test strip got seawater in it. It's damaged."

Guy visibly begins to relax. He reaches out and places his hand around my elbow. Nerves begin to spread through my body.

"Why didn't you say anything to me?" he asks.

I shrug. "Until I know for sure, there is nothing to tell."

"How late are you?"

"Over a week," I sheepishly answer.

He pensively looks around and absorbs his surroundings while he thinks. "So, you could just be late."

"I could be late," I confirm. "I've never been late before, but I could just be late."

He looks down at my belly. "I guess time will tell then."

I nod in agreement, stunned that he gave up on arguing with me and isn't insanely upset.

"Just don't keep anything from me. I can't help you if you don't let me."

"You're not mad?" I ask as I assess the confusion and hurt in his eyes.

He waves his hand out, palm up, still looking perplexed. "I just … I am mad that you tried to keep it from me." He pointedly stares at me. "But it's not like you did this on purpose."

I stop my eyes from rolling back. "Guy, I kind of did do this on purpose."

Realization hits him, and his jaw tenses. "Right. Let's get the fuck out of here. Let's find something to eat. I'll catch something." He storms off in front of me, making his way through the island's forest.

*What an asshole.*

I stomp behind him. "Oh, now, you're mad? You're mad that my husband and I wanted to get pregnant? That's what upsets you?"

He continues to walk with me trailing close behind. "Naomi, stop being such a brat. I'm not mad. It is what it is."

I wish I could believe his words, but his tone gave him away.

"We have only been on this island for three weeks. How can you so easily forget that we're both married?"

He stops and turns toward me, grabbing my arm. I don't budge. I let him hold on.

"What the fuck difference does it make? You're married." He takes a step closer to me. "I'm married." He inches in closer to my face. "But not here. That was another world."

I know what he's saying. Our old lives don't matter anymore because we might not ever go back to them. I've been battling with hope ever since the plane began to fall out of the sky.

"I can't give up," I say softly, looking into his now-gentle eyes.

He quickly lets go of me and turns to continue walking, breaking twigs and crunching leaves in his path. "Eventually, you're gonna have to. Whether you like it or not, you're stuck with me."

I run up to catch him and shove him in his broad back. I barely make an impact. He only slightly leans forward before turning around to face me again.

"That's what you want, isn't it?" I yell at him. "You want to be stuck here with me? You want me to give up hope?"

"I *want* you to deal with reality, Naomi!" he screams back.

With all my might, I take the air that I've sucked in my lungs and use it to punch out my words. "I. Love. My. Husband."

"Oh, come on." He throws his head back. "You are so self-centered. You think I care about whether or not you love your husband? You think that's what this is about? He's gone," he roars. "I'm here. Get fucking used to it."

"Don't treat me like I'm stupid, Guy. I know."

"You don't know shit," he spits back at me.

"I know that you have feelings for me, but you're wrong. You're just confused since we're stranded here together. I'm your only choice. It has nothing to do with me."

"Ooh," he slowly draws out. "Now, don't you treat me like I'm stupid. And don't pretend like you don't feel anything for me."

He calmly steps in front of me again and reaches out, touching my arm. His breathing slows, becoming controlled and meticulous with each breath. "I can see your body tremble inside when I touch you." He moves his hand up higher, closer to my shoulder, and stares at my chest. "I can see your nipples harden when my hands continue to move across your skin." He steps in even closer, moving his hand across my back, creating wakes of shivers in its path.

He leans toward my ear, and I can smell his masculinity. I feel a pulse deep inside me, making my whole body beat with anticipation.

"And I can feel your pussy throb when we're close like this."

"No." I look up to him with confidence I don't have but am trying to find. "You make me uncomfortable." I slowly push him away.

"You're full of shit. I turn you on." His cocky voice taunts me.

I start to walk away, covering my arms and shoulders, suddenly feeling very exposed. "Can't you just leave me alone?" I turn toward him and give my closing statement in this uncomfortable situation. "You're just a womanizing asshole, looking for his next extramarital lay, and I'm the closest thing to you."

Just as he has been wanting to suck the hope out of me—the hope of being rescued—I can see the hope drain from his face. Just what did he have in mind? I don't know, and I'm sure I don't care. But something leaves me feeling remorseful. My arms remain wrapped around myself; this time, it's for comfort. I try not to make any sounds as I cry, walking away from him.

Charles and I never fought much. There was never anything to fight about. Everything felt easy, and whatever decision we did make, it was catered to at every turn. Our life together was so simple. We never had any hardships worth fighting over.

I watch Guy circle around the fire, probing it with a long, broken-off tree branch. We haven't said a word to each other the past several hours since our argument. I wish I could have my space from him, but Guy and I don't have that option here. We've only been stewing in our disappointment and anger, being near each other.

The fire sparks after Guy pokes it again. I can't tell if he's bored or if he's resisting the urge to talk.

We sat in silence while we ate, and we continue to sit in silence while we wait. I think we're waiting for two very different things. Every now and then, from my peripheral, I catch him looking my way, but when I turn my head, he stares back into the fire, as if he's in a deep conversation with it.

I take my chances, and I turn to look at him. I want to tell him I'm sorry. I lost my temper, and my manners went flying out the door when he provoked me by blatantly coming on to me. He bends his knees and kneels down, crouching behind the orange wall of heat. He looks stronger now than when I first saw him, looking so dapper and clean on the plane. He's a totally different man now. It's crazy how a couple of weeks can change you so dramatically.

*Maybe I've changed, too?*

I've been looking at him too long, and now, I'm caught. He turns his head, and our eyes latch on to each other. I want to tell him a million things through my eyes, and I feel as if he's answering back, but we still don't actually speak.

He stands up and walks ten feet to where I'm sitting on the other side of the fire.

"Did you get enough to eat?" he asks and sits in the sand next to me.

I nod. "Thank you."

We both look out onto the dark ocean and matching sky with sprinkles of stars splayed across it.

With all the silence around us again, Guy breaks it when he asks, "Is that what you really think of me? A womanizing asshole?"

I stop and think, rehashing my words in my mind.

"How could you judge me like that? You're the only woman you've actually seen me around. Am I a womanizing asshole to you?"

"I'm sorry about what I said."

Truly, I don't want to hurt his feelings. It's just that he makes me so frustrated and angry, and I say things I might not mean.

"You didn't answer my question." He turns to look at my profile as I'm still staring out in the blank space ahead.

"I'll answer your question if I can start with an apology." I turn and look into his dark gray eyes, only illuminated by the nearby firelight. "I'm so sorry if I hurt you. You-you just scare me sometimes, and I don't react well."

"How do I scare you?" he asks calmly, concerned.

I breathe in and look away from his eyes, needing to concentrate on an honest answer. "I just have this really intense and nervous feeling around you, and I'm afraid of what it means. I don't even know what it means. I know who I am, but I feel like a different person with you than when I'm with …" I trail off, not wanting to dive any further into these thoughts.

My frustration starts to build. "I just feel like you have the wrong idea. Tell me I'm wrong, Guy. Tell me you don't have feelings for me." I turn and look into his gray eyes, trying not to concentrate on his luscious pink lips sitting in a nest of his short dark brown facial hairs.

"I don't know what I feel, Naomi. I just know it's not because you're the closest woman to me. Maybe I do care about you more than a married man should. Maybe I care about you more than any man should. Call it what you want, but I've never felt so strongly about anyone."

"This isn't how you felt when you met—"

Guy cuts my words off in their track, "Marina? No. I thought she was beautiful, and that's about it. You're beautiful, too, but …"

He looks at me, and his fingers twitch, as if he wants to reach out and touch me. I feel goose bumps all over and begin to rub my hands up and down my arms.

"You're more than that."

I look down and blush. "No, Guy. I was gonna ask if it compares to how you felt about the woman you cheated on Marina with."

His face swells with disappointment. "Look, I can't change my past, and I shouldn't have to defend it either. All I can tell you is that it's not who I am anymore, and it felt justified at the time."

I breathe in deep. For some reason, I believe him; I do. It's just easier to push him away sometimes. I'm finding it hard to balance relying on him to live here until we're rescued and depending on him to fill a void. A deep, unfulfilled void. It would be so easy for him to fill it.

I find myself trying to justify it more and more with every day that passes.

# Sixteen

Seven more days means we've been here for twenty-seven days.

After Guy finished taking a bath in the cascading pool, I got in. It feels so good to get clean with what feels like fresh water, and the peacefulness of floating in the bright blue pool takes me to another place. For a few moments, I can relax as if I were in a dreamlike scenario.

The wind that blows through the trees and ruffles the leaves on the branches are singing to me instead of mocking me and pestering my existence here. This is my one sanctuary, and Guy has been leaving me alone to enjoy it in solitude each day.

As I float on my back, the small waves created by the waterfall tickle at the sides of my breasts and roll over the bush between my legs. The sky darkens, and a gray cloud, the color of Guy's eyes, passes over and shields me from the sun. Another gust of wind tells me a storm is likely coming.

*Good.* We need the fresh rainwater. It's been over ten days since it last rained.

"Naomi!" I can almost make out Guy's voice, but it's muffled by the water submerging my ears.

The foliage violently sways away from each other, creating a part in the middle. He's getting close, and he's still calling my name.

"Guy, go away! I'm not done yet."

But nothing changes. It's imminent; he's going to appear any moment through the lush leaves.

"I'm naked! Leave me alone until I'm dressed."

I look around, and I'm completely exposed in the middle of the pool. My clothes are off to the side, hanging over a thick, perpendicular branch, but I'd like to dry a little before putting them back on. I'm trapped.

His masculine, bare chest appears, supported by burly legs. His virility grows each day. My nipples harden, and my insides shake. I want to hide and cover myself, but all I can do is cross my arms and place my hands over my breasts.

"Guy, what is your problem? I told you, I'm not done yet." I try to stand my ground with confidence, but really, I feel like melting into the pool beneath me.

His chest heavily puffs up and down. "Naomi," flies out of his mouth with a sense of urgency.

Just one word mixed with his tone is enough for me to forget that I'm naked. Still, his eyes scan me up and down before focusing back on my face. Something big is happening.

"What is it?" I ask between my own breaths of heavy air.

"It's a ship. Let's go." He immediately turns and runs back the way he came.

I quickly splash and paddle with my arms until I'm close enough to the pool's shore to run. I grab my clothes, hopping on one foot as I step into my loose-fitting skirt. Throwing my shirt—it's so big on me now that there is no need to button and unbutton it, as it just slides on—over my head, I pick up speed to catch up to Guy.

He is only a few yards ahead of me, but when I break through the trees into the open space of sand, we both stop in our tracks.

I begin screaming, jumping, and waving my arms.

Guy jolts, as if he's about to join me in flagging down the ship off in the distance, but he stops himself. "It's too far. I thought it was moving toward us, but it's not. It's moving away."

"But we have to try," I beg.

He pivots on his feet and runs back toward the firepit he made outside of our hut. "I'll make a fire."

He's been trying to have a constant, controlled burn throughout the day, so he doesn't need to start a new burn every evening.

Although the ship is merely a blip in the distance, I continue to wail and cry, "Help! Help! We're here!"

Guy throws log after log—he's been compiling them over the weeks—on top of the small, burning branches. He grabs a large palm tree leaf and begins to fan, building momentum for the fire to feed on oxygen and wood.

"This isn't going to work," he says while controlling the palm leaf up and down. "They're too far away."

"Shut up!" I scream back to him. "They have to see us. It's time. It's time they found us."

I know he's right. Deep down, I know that ship isn't going to see us, and we are going to be right back where we've been every day since we washed up here, but I just don't want to hear his logic.

The ship gets smaller and smaller in the distance.

"It's too late. They're too far gone."

"Nooooo!" I scream.

And something takes over me. Some kind of suicidal demon grabs ahold of me, and my mind goes blank. My body reacts on autopilot, and I'm running for my life toward the boat I know I can't catch.

I can hear my feet slapping against the shallow water, but I feel nothing. My focus is on that little tiny dot that is supposed to be my savior. Guy's voice becomes background noise to the water that's now rising up to my hips … and I'm not slowing down. Once I've run far enough for the water to be up to my breasts, I take a little hop and dive my head under.

*I'll swim all the way if I have to.*

Something grabs my foot and yanks my efforts to a halt. Under the water, I turn and see Guy grabbing on to me. I fight him. I kick with my other foot and flail about, but he tightens his grip and reaches up further until he has a solid hold on my hips. He pushes off the ocean floor, and we burst above water. His grasp on me tightens with every move I make to fend him off.

"Let go of me!" I push him and try to pull myself underwater again.

"Naomi, don't do this. It's too late. It's gone."

"No." I continue to fight him, but I'm losing strength.

I try punching him, but I barely land my fist on his jaw. He simply turns his head, and my knuckles only brush past his cheek. He takes both hands and turns me to face away from him, securely hugging me around my middle. He's struggling to keep a tight grip while holding us both above water.

"Stop fighting me!" he screams in my ear.

His muscles clench around my body even tighter. It only tires me more to fight, but I keep trying to kick him off me and push myself farther out into the ocean, like I'm possessed.

"It's gone," he says, gasping for air with his head grapples to stay above water. "Ahhh!" Guy's cry startles me back to reality. "Ahhh!" he yells again, letting go of me and crunching his body down around his shin.

Instincts suddenly kick in. I dive underwater and grab his arm, yanking him away from retreating thin and delicate tentacles a few feet behind him.

When I touch him, his eyes spring open and lock on to mine.

*Help me. Move!* I try to plea with him.

His face grimaces as he tries to move. I pull him up, and he swats his arms in the water as best he can to get us to the surface.

We gasp for air in unison as our heads emerge from the water.

I roll on my back and kick my legs as hard as I can, holding on to Guy's upper body. Now that he's floating above the water, I can get us closer to shallow water.

As soon as I know my feet can touch, I stand up and push through the water's resistance, heaving and pulling Guy's weakening body behind me.

It takes the last bit of strength I have to pull him onto the sand, completely out of the water.

"I'm so sorry," I shriek, bending over him. "I don't know what got into me. I'm so sorry. What have I done?"

"Ahhh," he calls out in pain, not able to respond to me.

Seeing him like this brings a dark cloud of fear over me.

*What have I done? Guy, I don't want to hurt you.*

Something heavy pulls in my chest.

Guy remains on his back, his forehead covered in sweat beads.

"What can I do?"

He struggles to move his head back and forth. "Clean it," comes out in a strained, raspy whisper.

I look down to his shin that he's holding and see three welts, all different sizes. His leg looks like it got beat with a whip, and the welts seem to be swelling by the second.

"Okay, okay." I get up and run back to our hut as fast as I can.

Grabbing two cups of rainwater, I try not to spill them or stumble as I rush back to Guy. I only pause for a moment, making sure I aim over the wounds on his shin before pouring the water.

Guy grunts, but I'm happy to see the water wash away a lot of the sand and dirt. His breathing becomes slow and harsh as he focuses on controlling the pain.

"Was it a jellyfish?"

"I think so," he barely gets out.

Several more lines and welts begin to appear, some wrapping around the curve of his leg.

"So, you'll be okay then, right?"

Guy reaches over and pats the top of my hand. "It'll be okay." He hardly finishes speaking before rolling on his side and vomiting into the sand. "I'll be fine," he squeaks out.

"My poor guy," I whisper down to him. "Let's get you into the hut, so I can take care of you. Can you use your other leg to push back and help me drag you?"

He nods, and we start moving him back. Our hut is only about twenty yards up the shore before the tree line, but it's a painful and laborious trek.

Once I get him fully under cover of our hut's roof, I settle in beside him.

"What is the pain like?" I ask, moving my hand across his face and looking down on him.

His head moves into my hand, letting its weight rest in my palm.

"It burns," he says with his eyes closed. "But it'll be fine." His eyes spring open. "I'm so sorry," he tells me.

"Why on earth would you be sorry? This is all my fault."

"I'm sorry we didn't get rescued. But I promise, it'll be okay. I'll make sure it's okay for us."

"Shh. All I care about is that you're okay. That's all that matters right now."

He doesn't respond to me, just continues to say, "If you're pregnant, I'll make sure your baby is safe, too. I know I can make this work for us. If we have to." His voice fades away.

# Seventeen

I could hardly sleep. Every few minutes, I had to sit up and check on Guy. His leg continues to look worse. The skin has broken, exposing his wound on the first welt that appeared in the middle of his shin. So far, that seems to be the mark that's the most severe.

Guy moans and tries to move his upper body.

"What is it? What's wrong?"

"My back," he groans. His hand moves to his lower back, but he doesn't seem to be able to move enough to show me exactly where.

"What can I do?"

"Nothing, Nay," he quietly says and drifts back to sleep.

I feel so helpless.

I can't even say that I woke up because I'm not sure I got any sleep to begin with. It's been two nights, and all I can think about is what more I can do for Guy.

Somewhere between when he got stung and now, I gave up hope on ever being rescued. At this moment, I don't even care about real food, Manhattan, or any civilization. All I care about is Guy being okay.

Rolling over so that my face is hovering above his, I study his breathing. It's even and calm but coming out in short intervals. I can feel the heat radiating off his body.

I put the back of my hand to his forehead. He's burning up. Looking down at his leg, I can see why. His largest gash seems to be infected. The other marks on his leg don't seem to be getting worse, so I hope he'll start to get better now.

Maybe this is the worst of it.

"Guy," I say softly.

"Hmm?" he hums, keeping his eyes closed.

"You have a fever. Can you drink more water?"

He tries to shake his head, but it hardly moves. "There's not enough," he mumbles.

"It's overcast today. I'll get more."

I reach up and grab our last saved cup of rainwater. I put the rim of the banana leaf to his lips. My other hand scoops around the back of his neck, and I help him sit up just a little.

After he takes a sip, his body immediately relaxes back to lie down.

"I need to get you some food," I whisper in his ear.

He barely nods. Keeping his eyes shut, he says, "You're going to be a great mom, Naomi."

He's delirious from his fever. But that still feels really good to hear. I quietly smile at him before leaving the hut.

I grab a large stick to help me hike and strike branches out of the way. I need to go a little deeper into the center of the island where the bananas are riper.

Skipping from one rock to another, I can't help but smirk at myself.

*Who am I?* I wonder as I trek along a desolate island, barefoot, hunting food. I've become this woman who can survive on her own in dire circumstances.

A knot forms in my throat when a realization hits me. I don't need Guy for survival, like I once thought I did. I'm capable of doing this on my own … but I don't want to.

Even being away from him now makes me miss him. It's only been a few minutes, and I'm longing for his scent and piercing gray eyes.

I swallow that knot in my throat and move faster, wanting to get back to him as soon as possible and give him food that will hopefully help him get stronger. But there needs to be more. There has to be something more I can do for him.

It would be so convenient if I could just trip over penicillin mold. I stop and look around, thinking something has got to hit me. There has got to be some natural remedy in this forest that can help him. I shake my head at myself. I don't even know what penicillin mold looks like. I wouldn't even know if one plant or another was poisonous. And the last thing I want is to hurt Guy even more. But, as I think to myself, I notice that I'm staring at something. A vegetation sprouting from the ground with thick, pointed leaves circling in a spiral. It almost looks like a fat artichoke.

*I know this plant.*

When I vacationed with my family as a girl, my mother showed me this plant once. She broke a leaf in half and rubbed its oil on my sunburn.

I rush over to it and snatch a leaf. I snap it in half, just like my mom did, and I can see the pores inside the moist, delicate flesh of the leaf oozing out its oil.

*This is aloe!*

I break off several of the plant's limbs. If I need more, I know where to find it.

I still need to get him food.

As soon as I find the fruit that's ripe enough, I grab what I need and turn around to head back.

Lugging a fifteen-pound vine of bananas over my shoulder, I gently place them down next to our hut and gingerly step inside with the aloe.

He's asleep, mumbling between breaths. I can feel the heat from his body as I near.

When I crouch down, I first assess his leg. No change from earlier. Then, I place the back of my hand on his forehead. Still very warm.

I snap a leaf, making sure he gets the freshest moisture from it, and I gently rub it on. After I cover all the red and irritated marks on his leg, I sit back on my heels and hope it helps. That's about all I can do.

He stirs and slurs out my name.

"I'm here," I tell him, brushing his disheveled hair away from his eyes. "I brought bananas."

"No, you," he mutters. "I want you, Naomi."

His head stirs, and his eyes flutter open to a very thin line, but I know he sees me. I place my hands on each side of his face. His scent, the sliver of gray eyes I can see, his rugged jawline, Guy in this vulnerable state—it all heightens my attraction and pull toward him.

I can't help myself. I lean in and press my lips on his.

"Naomi," he softly says while our lips are still touching.

But I pull away.

I've crossed a line.

"I shouldn't have done that," I whisper, looking down on him.

But his eyes are closed, and he looks as if he's asleep again.

I start to hear the rain hitting the banana leaves around our hut. Perfect. Now, we'll have more drinking water and more clean water to wash Guy's wounds with.

It's been the same routine Guy had in place for us before he got hurt and sick. I get up, and we eat bananas and coconuts. If there aren't any saved from the day before, I go out and find some. I've even climbed trees to knock down the freshest coconuts. Then, in the afternoon, I spear a fish from the lagoon on the back side of the island.

Only I'm doing this all on my own. Every morning and evening, I apply more aloe, and it seems to be working.

After three more days of him being sick, his fever finally broke, and the gash on his leg finally closed up. It still looks very irritated and inflamed, but every day, it's getting better.

Guy is sitting up now, moving around. Even though he's healthier each day, he's still low on energy.

We lie in our hut, facing each other. I brush my hand over his face, clearing away any strands of hair that have fallen over his eyes. We stare at each other for a few minutes as the night goes from dark to very dark.

"I would have died if you weren't here to take care of me."

That reminds me, I need to apply more aloe. I sit up and grab a fresh piece.

"Shh," I soothe as I start to rub the green leaf over his shin. "Don't talk like that. It's my fault you got hurt in the first place. I don't know why I went out there. I lost my mind for a bit." I tell him sincerely, "I'm sorry."

His hand covers mine, stilling it on his leg. "I don't blame you for what happened. You don't deserve this. You should be in New York, helping kids have a better life. I wish you didn't have to be stuck here with me."

I move my hand. My eyes look away from him, and I stare down at the hard wooden floor we're lying on. "We're never going to be rescued. I realize that now. And I wouldn't want to be here without you."

"Come here." He urges me closer.

I scoot in, resting my head on his chest, while he pulls me closer with one arm around me.

"You don't deserve to be here either," I say into the rough hairs on his chest.

"Yes, I do," he says softly. "I haven't led the most honest life."

"What are you talking about?"

He takes a deep breath, making my head move up with his chest. "I told you, I found a way to pay for my private high school and then again in college."

"Yes."

"I sold Adderall to students," he confesses.

I hate that it doesn't surprise me. He already told me they were poor, and a teenager's salary wouldn't be able to support prep-school tuition.

"I wanted to conquer the world," he continues. "I hated being poor. I hated that my mother and brother were poor, and I felt like I was better than everyone else around me. I knew I couldn't get into Harvard for their business program if I graduated from public school, even with a GPA over 4.0. I also knew my mom couldn't afford to send me to a private school."

My fingers run across his chest hairs as I listen.

"I worked at a grocery store and saved enough to pay the first two months of tuition, but I knew that was all I could do. Once I started at my new school, I felt like I was finally among kids like me. Desperate kids, but they were desperate for a different reason. They wanted to live up to their parents' expectations. That meant good grades. They needed to stay up all night, studying. I knew a guy who could get Adderall, so I became the prep-school dealer."

"Did you use?"

"No—at least, not in high school. I worked hard, but the curriculum seemed to be easier for me than others."

"But you used in college?"

I feel his chest move when he nods.

"Just a few times before tests. In college, it wasn't just Adderall. I sold harder stuff, too, because I needed to make a lot more money. I even had enough saved up to stop as soon as I graduated."

I sit up higher, facing Guy, and look into his eyes. "It wasn't your fault," I tell him. "The system doesn't work for kids like you … yet," I add, "you made it work the only way you knew how. It wasn't your fault."

His hand moves up and gently rubs my back. "It was my fault. I did what I had to do. But it was wrong. I'm still trying to make it right."

"How?" I simply ask.

He breathes in through his nose before saying, "I started several scholarship programs for underprivileged kids."

I softly smile, staring at his lips, remembering what they felt like. "You and I aren't so different."

Guy's eyes move down, and I can tell he's staring at my lips, too. Just before I feel the need to inch closer, he turns his head.

"No, we're very different, Nay. I love that you're a better person than I am. But I'm trying."

I lie back down on his chest, forgetting what I just thought about doing. *I'm still married*, I remind myself.

"I think I'm feeling strong enough to start walking around tomorrow," he says as I close my eyes.

"That's a good idea."

"One more time," he grunts.

I throw his arm over the back of my shoulders and try to hoist him up. All his weight is on his good leg as he stands here with me, focusing and readying himself for the pain.

He takes a sharp inhale through his nose, and then he steps on his injured leg. "Ahhh," he yells as he quickly moves all his weight back to his good leg. He breathes heavy as he tries the cycle again, this time taking more pressure off me and supporting his own weight.

After four steps, he collapses on the ground, and I fall with him.

"It's okay," I remind him. "You're doing great. It's better each time you try."

I can still see the pain on his face, but he tries to laugh.

"Ha. It's like teaching a baby how to walk for the first time."

We both hear the word *baby* and become quiet and reflective.

I lean over, placing my head on his shoulder, needing him to support me now. After a few moments of silence, I ask Guy, "Did you ever think about having kids?"

I feel his jaw move, and I know he's smiling.

"I did," he says, as if I should be surprised. "But I never thought about it with Marina. She never brought it up, and I never had the desire to raise children with her."

"But you still thought about having kids."

His shoulder moves slightly, trying to shrug. "Yes, I think I did feel like kids were in my future. I guess, deep down, I always knew Marina and I wouldn't be together forever."

"Hmm …"

"What?"

"I think it's funny that you thought more about kids outside your marriage rather than for your marriage."

"Yes," he agrees. I can feel him nod. "I don't think kids and marriage have to go hand in hand. Honestly?" He moves his head, so he can see my reaction.

I smile at him, wanting to hear everything he has to tell me. The more I learn about Guy Harrington, the more fascinating I find him.

"Tell me."

He tilts his head to touch mine, and we both look out at the water in front of us.

"I've always wanted to adopt. There are too many kids out there who need better lives."

I can't help but beam. This man is far from the person I first thought he was. Yes, he's strong, masculine, and capable, but he's so much more. At first, he used his brute strength and stubborn attitude to cover the genuine heart I now know is inside him. But not anymore. Now, I get the whole Guy. And I get him all to myself.

Guy moves his lips to the side of my head and just lightly moves them back and forth without putting any pressure. I feel like he wants to say something, but the moment passes us. And I'm relieved. I want him too badly to resist him right now.

With a swollen heart and a need that seems to be starving for Guy's touch, I force myself to stand, pulling him up with me. "Let's try again."

He nods and hops to my side. But, instead of throwing his arm around the back of my shoulders, he reaches over and holds my hand. I squeeze around his palm.

"You can do this," I reassure him.

I can see the look of anticipation on his face as he braces himself for the pain, but he keeps his eyes on me. We stare at each other as we take a step.

*One, two, three, four, five.*

Five steps, almost completely supporting his own weight. I call that progress.

I've found a new meaning to the word *team*. Never before have I been so in sync with someone. Our bond is growing stronger each day.

Guy is walking with a limp but getting stronger every time he leaves the hut. He even ran yesterday. He's going to be just fine.

I've also found a new strength and energy I never knew was in me.

We're adding on to our hut and making it bigger. We now have a living room—at least, that is what I call it. It's no Manhattan penthouse apartment, but it's feeling more like home with each improvement we make.

I helped Guy make a hammock. It's been more comfortable, sleeping there. Ripping vines and palm branches was a workout, and now, Guy isn't the only one building more muscle tone. Back at home, I never worked out. I've never had a gym membership. I have a natural slender figure, but I haven't participated in sports since high school.

If only Charles could see me now—how strong I've become. I'm not sure if he would smile and laugh and hope things would go back to the way they used to be or if he would be proud and encourage me to continue growing stronger.

Guy is proud. It is in his eyes, the way he gazes at me from afar, and the intensity I feel when we're only a few feet away. He's noticing my new form, and he's showing so much self-control because I know it turns him on. His eyes narrow, his breathing deepens, and his pants bulge. Slowly, I've developed my own pride in how I can make him react. Still, I try to keep my distance physically. I might have lost hope in ever getting off this island, but I have not lost my wedding vows. I will forever be committed to Charles.

"I'm going for a walk," I inform Guy while he's chipping away at a branch, creating a spear for catching more fish.

"Careful, Nay."

I smile at him as I walk past. "Of course." I brush my hand against his, giving him reassurance that I'm considering his words. The contact gives me my own sense of reassurance.

It takes less than an hour to walk around the entire perimeter of the island. I double that by moseying around and admiring the little things. Things I never bothered to appreciate before. Like how the water is always more still on the other side where the shoreline curves in, creating a small, shallow peninsula.

It's been easier for us to fish on this side. Something I discovered while Guy was sick.

I've almost come full circle when I think to explore where the pool and waterfall are coming from in the middle of the island. I trace my steps back a few yards to where a thin stream of water escapes inland. I follow it like a hound dog trailing a scent.

Just inside the tropical foliage off the sandy shore, it disappears under the muddy terrain of an uprooted dead tree and marshy plants. Where the tall tree fell over, vibrant green leaves, bushes, and wild plant life flourish in its wake.

I push past the exposed trunk and darting roots to walk along the stalk of the tree, following this lush vegetation. This path I'm on has gotten more moisture than the rest of the small forest. Its nutrients and water are coming from more than just rainfall.

Two hundred more feet in, I find what I've been looking for. All the thriving plants have been covering up the stream that leads to the pools and cascading waterfall. The water coming in from the ocean is slow, but it's steady. Rocks and boulders create a dam, creating the first of the two pools. At one corner, the water spills over and falls from rock to rock until it meets the bottom pool that Guy and I have been using to bathe and swim.

I've never seen anything so beautiful before.

Bending down, I brace myself behind a tree thicker than my whole body.

*Oh shit, this is overwhelming.*

I curve around, so I'm hidden, taking a moment to collect my scattered thoughts and racing heart.

*Breathe, Naomi. Breathe. He's just a man*, I try to tell myself.

But, no, that is unlike any man I've ever seen before. I can't help but need another peek, instantly addicted to this rush and pulsing blood pumping through me.

Throbbing starts beating between my legs as I eye his tight, naked ass. Perfectly shaped and firm. He ducks down into the water, allowing his entire head to go under, but then he pops up and wipes the dripping water away from his face. He runs his hands through his hair, and he walks in the opposite direction of me, out of the shallow end of the pool. He must be done with his swim.

Seeing him naked in that water reminds me of when I touched myself. My hands and fingers feel as if they weren't my own, and they want to play with me again. I take a step closer and shield myself behind the next nearest tree.

My God, my body is screaming at me, telling me I want this man so badly, but my heart is telling me to walk away. More like telling me to run in the other direction. My body wins out, and I take another step closer. Curiosity is overruling me now.

I have no sense that he knows I'm here, but he turns in my direction, giving me a full frontal view. My hand goes up toward my throat, as if I were catching my breath in its tracks. It's the same shock and surprise I felt when I first met Guy. He was fully clothed then. This is much more of an impact.

My gasp is audible and catches Guy's attention. Just before his body moves fast enough to look my way, I hide myself behind the tree, my chest heaving with adrenaline.

"Nay?" he calls out, but uncertainty clouds his voice. He doesn't know I'm here; he's only testing.

I stand still until I can hear his movements in the water again.

I move closer; I'm only about ten yards away from him. As I crouch down to his hip-level, my eyes fixate on his large cock between his legs.

I don't think I've ever thought to use the word *cock* until I met Guy. Charles and I have never spoken to each other like that. But I can't think of a better word to call it. It's everything that masculinity should be.

Towering over the water, which is only resting above his knees, Guy goes back to his bathing routine and bends down, soaking his hips and abdomen. He uses his hands to wash off any dirt that might be clinging on to his skin. First, his legs, and now, his cock. His hands wrap around its girth, and he strokes it. Then, he gathers up water from the pool and strokes over it again.

I feel wet between my legs. Moisture is building and pooling low inside me and seeping out, soaking my inner thighs. I look down to witness this reaction I'm having, but before I can investigate, I hear Guy calling me again.

"Naomi."

Still, I sit silent, hoping he doesn't realize I'm here.

"Naomi." His voice rises, louder and more confident. "Naomi, I know you're there. What are you doing?"

*Fuck. I've been caught.*

*Shit. Shit. Shit.*

I take a quick moment to plan my next move. I'll just have to act as if I just walked up on him.

I take a step, crackling branches below my feet. "Oh, hi, Guy." I turn the corner from the tree I've been hiding behind and quickly cover my eyes. "Oh God, I'm so sorry. I didn't realize you didn't have your clothes on."

Between my fingers, I see his hands slap up in the air and down to his sides.

"Oh, for fuck's sake, Naomi. I know you were watching me."

"I was not," I say, defending myself, slapping my own hands down to my sides. I breathe in heavy, having another look at his bare, virile body. I've never felt so desperate to be filled.

He turns to leave the water, and he grabs his clothes, easily stepping into his ragged pants.

*Hold it together, Naomi,* I tell myself while gathering strength to get past this horrifically embarrassing moment. I want to go crawl under a rock somewhere and hide.

When he steps toward me, I attempt to step past him.

"I'm sorry. I didn't mean to intrude. I followed a stream here, and I want to go back to the hut."

He doesn't let me pass. "Wait. Can we talk about this? I know you were watching me."

"There is nothing to talk about." I move my head to try to look past him for the best path out of here, but he dodges my view. "It was just a mistake, and I'm sorry."

His anger sparks. "You're not sorry. I know you were watching me."

I push to try to escape, but he holds on to my shoulders.

"So what?" I try to confidently throw my words at him.

His eyes study my face and seductively move down as he loosens his grip on me. I don't run for it like I intended. I allow him to look at me as I was just looking at him with no clothes on. I do the same but imagine I'm looking at his bare cock again, which is now hiding under his pants.

I swallow hard. "I can't do this. I have to go," I tell him and try to spin on my heels to walk away.

He doesn't immediately try to stop me this time. Then, he reaches out and grabs my hand as I pass, and everything changes inside me.

# Nineteen

"I can't *not* do this anymore," he says, rolling his fingers around my palm and jerking me back to him.

He embraces me in a way that forces our faces to be only inches from each other, and he reaches his hand up to caress my hair out of my eyes. "I've reached my limit," he says into my mouth.

His words are powerful and come with a certain determination. I want nothing more than to succumb to it. But even more power comes from the intensity exuding from his eyes, searching into mine for an answer. If I don't speak, I know he'll find it there. And, if he doesn't like what I have to say, I'm not sure he'll care or turn back.

All my willpower and the consequences I've feared drain out of my body. I'm left with nothing but my desire for him to touch me, hold me, and fill me with everything he has to give.

"I've reached my limit, too," I confess, taking my last breath free of his mouth.

We desperately touch our lips together, smashing into each other as if it were something we'd needed all our lives, as if I never tried so hard to resist it.

The sweet release of tension eases my body and readies me for him. He's captured my mouth, and I'm savoring every flavor I can suck out of him. He tastes even better inside than when I pressed my lips to his over a week ago. The flavor is divine, but I still need more. I trust he'll give it to me as he eagerly possesses my body with his hands.

*Guy. Guy. Guy*, is all I can think about.

He's all I can think about feeling right now.

While still devouring my mouth, he reaches down and pulls the hem of my shirt up. I reach my arms in the air and allow the garment to pass over my head. More of his skin on my skin—this is all I want at this very second … but more of it.

His lips leave mine and drift over below my ear and down my neck, sucking and savoring in his path. His kiss goes deeper than skin; it excites my nerves and quickens my blood flow.

I feel out of body as he continues his path down to my breasts. He only pauses for a short moment before running his finger over my hard nipple; he tugs before putting it in his mouth. The excitement springs through my whole body and makes me throb, the pulse coming from between my legs. It's as if my body is calling to him.

"You're so perfect, Nay. I've needed you for so long now," he mumbles into my skin as he sucks and explores even more, igniting parts inside me I didn't know existed. He rises back up to my mouth. "Tell me you want me," he demands.

I know my heart wants to say *no*, but my body and mind scream, *Yes, I want you!* I can't even hear my heart anymore. The sound of my need is too loud. I'll do anything to fulfill it.

"Yes, yes, I want you." I beg him for more.

Faster than I can blink, he tugs the rim of my skirt down. It easily falls to the ground.

Grabbing my bare ass, he hoists me into his arms, and I instinctively wrap my legs around his waist while I kiss him as hard as I want him to fuck me at this very moment.

I'm so obvious. How can he not see how badly I want him? I *need* him.

As he carries me, I can feel my wetness against his abdomen. Never leaving my mouth, he takes strong, wide strides around the pool to the cascading waterfall.

A few feet up and just to the side of the running water, he lays me down on a flat rock with a trickle of water running over it. We're at the opposite side of the pool from where I was watching him. My legs are open at his hip level. All he needs to do is take off his pants, so he can slide into me, and my world will be complete.

I bend my knees and prop my elbows up. Our eyes are locked on to each other. He licks his fingertips—an unnecessary act, as I'm ready for whatever he can give me—and reaches down between my legs.

He tickles the folds around the outside with his thumb. I gasp from the excitable shock his touch gives me, and it's only the beginning. His eyes widen after seeing my reaction, and he appears possessed, narrowing his focus down on me even more.

He bends down, caressing my thighs with his hands, and he takes ahold of me, wrapping his hands around my hips and ass. He takes one more look into my eyes and then puts his face between my legs.

"Ahhh," I instantly cry out with wet pleasure bursting inside me.

Charles has never put his tongue inside me before. It's never appealed to either of us, but with one look from Guy, I knew exactly what he wanted to do, and I wanted him to do it to me.

"You taste so good. I've never tasted anything so perfect. I love your pussy," he says while he laps up my insides, moving the moisture to my clit.

It's overwhelming.

"Ahhh," I cry out again and squirm my hips up further to his mouth, pleading for more. I feel this urge to rock and thrust, but I'm also afraid to move and change what he's doing because whatever he is doing, he's doing it perfectly.

My body sings on the inside, and a cluster of intensity builds, higher and higher. Guy's focus never falters. My hand reaches down and grips his thick hair in my fingers. I want to pet him and reward him with the good job he's doing with my body, pleasing my core and making me mindless.

"Oh God, Guy, I'm gonna come," I inform him.

His ravenous hunger for me increases, and my blood quickens, pooling around my throbbing clit.

"Oh, oh," I cry with every movement he makes on me. *This is it.*

An explosion oozes from my core and spreads through my whole body, like warm butter on toast. I cry out his name as if I'm expelling Guy out of me with the pleasure. As the pulses slow and calm to a rolling ecstasy, I cry out his name again, this time thanking him for making my body quake and wail with satisfaction.

My body starts to relax, but I'm only partially satisfied. Guy comes up and puts his mouth on mine, his tongue taking in more of me. I can taste myself in his spit, and I lick it up in his mouth as if I were some sort of sexual beast, craving my own flavor.

"Fuck, Naomi. Oh fuck, you don't know what you do to me," he speaks while never breaking away from my mouth.

My satisfaction only lasts a moment. I'm still unfulfilled. I need more.

I reach down to his hard cock to show him that I know what I do to him. I can feel the effect I have on him. As soon as I touch him, trying to grip his girth around his pants fabric, Guy stands up, yanks his pants down, and lets his cock spring free without obstacle or restriction.

*Ah, there you are. Now that I've seen you, I want to feel you.*

Stepping out one leg at a time, he bends each knee on the rock, just to the outside of my hips. He grabs my back and pulls my upper body closer to his. Our lips touch and begin to devour each other again.

I can feel his stiffness between my legs. It's too far away. I reach down and direct it straight toward my opening.

"I want your cock," I tell him.

He doesn't need to answer. He just needs to continue to devour me and fill me.

At first touch, when his tip tickles the insides of my delicate flesh, Guy grabs across my ass with one hand and thrusts me onto him.

"Ohhh." The force and instant satisfaction makes me cry out.

He travels deep inside, hitting my back wall and forcing past what I thought were my limits, into a new place of gratification. I'm instantly addicted, and I want him to push into me again and again and again. He pumps and moves inside me, crashing through my barriers and taking me over. I've found something I can't live without—this feeling.

He can't stop, and I do nothing to show that I want anything less than more.

"Oh, Nay, you see what you do to me? Do you see how I need you?" Hearing his voice while he's deep inside me ignites every nerve in my whole body.

I can't respond to what he said. All I can do is cry out in joy and painfully good pleasure.

Sex has never been like this for me before. I always enjoyed when Charles and I made love, but this … this is fucking, and I never knew how badly I needed it.

Guy grips me under my ass and lifts me up to my feet. He spins me around, grabbing my neck and pulling my head back, keeping it close to his. He kisses my neck from behind while he places himself inside me again. His hand sprawls across my breasts, pushing me tight into him, giving him the leverage he needs to reach further inside me when he thrusts.

"Ohhh."

His kiss on my stretched out neck, under my ear, feels as deep as his cock inside me.

The penetration grows and builds into a solid foundation of sex that runs through my blood, tickling my whole body from the inside out. There is only one way for this to end. Only one way I'll ever let him stop fucking me.

"Oh God," I cry out.

My body has a mind of its own and seems to know exactly what I need. I need him deeper, and I have to move to get him there. I throw my torso down and place my hands on the rock in front of me. I stick my ass out further, so he can go deeper, deeper than I thought my body would allow. But it does. He fits so perfectly and creates titillating explosions in the back wall of my insides.

He has completely captured me in this position, and I'm powerless to his movements. I crave each one, and he holds all the cards to my imminent pleasure.

As he keeps thrusting into me, I can hear and feel his balls slapping on my taint, such sensitive flesh. I love the sound.

"Naomi," he calls out my name.

I can feel him tense and stiffen even further than he has been. He must be so close. I'm not sure if I can orgasm again yet.

"Oh, Nay, touch yourself," he says.

Instinctively, I follow his instructions without thinking, as if my life depended on it. I reach down with one hand and circle my fingers around my clit.

"Oh fuck," I can't help but say.

Sex is coming at me from every direction—the walls inside me, my taint, and now, my clit.

"Ohhh." I feel that buildup again. It's coming, and I'm coming with it.

Guy's fingers dig into the sides of my ass. He clenches every muscle in his hard body. Everything I've been working for since I gave in to him and first tasted his mouth is coming to a climax, and I need it. I rub my fingers around faster, and my body can't hold on anymore.

I start to convulse and spasm, spewing my internal explosions out in any way I can.

We cry out together, "Oh fuck," and "Ah!"

Guy screams my name, panting out of breath, and thrusts hard one last time. He holds it in me, leaving every drop he has inside me.

He falls on top of me and scoops me around to his side as he lies on his back.

*I want to be held.*

I have no idea if he knows I need to be held right now. His arm reaches past my shoulder blades, folding over me, and he pulls me snug into his side. His other hand reaches across his body to my left thigh, and he pulls my leg over on top of his chiseled abs. I couldn't be more held than I am right now. I breathe into the nook he's settled me into and embrace a feeling I never thought I would have after something like this—guiltless satisfaction.

Guy breathes deep, relaxing even further. "Naomi, you have no idea how long I've wanted that."

"I think I do know. Probably a little more than a month, right?" I smile and tilt my nose up under his chin.

His head subtly moves back and forth. "No, Naomi. It's been a lot longer than that. I've maybe wanted this my whole life. I just didn't know it was you until I met you."

I sharply breathe in and silently process what he said. I can't find the words to come up with a response. I know how my body feels, but I still can't hear what my heart has to say about it all.

# Twenty

The guilt I thought I would feel is far off in the distance—maybe as far as Manhattan. It's still there, but it's far enough away that I can live with myself. Thoughts of Charles do pass through my mind, but at this point, all I can think about is how I truly want him to be happy. I wonder if he will ever move on from me. Would he be angry, knowing that I moved on, knowing that he wasn't an option for me anymore?

I prop my hand under my chin and look up to Guy's face. "That was the first time I've ever come during sex," I confess.

His hand moves up and down my naked back. "I know. I wanted to give that to you." His chin moves down, and he places his lips on my forehead, kissing me tenderly and sweetly. It seems new but strangely familiar.

"I never thought I would end up like this with you," I say quietly, deep in thought.

Guy doesn't say anything.

"When we first met, I mean. You were in such a bad mood, and I convinced myself I didn't like you at all."

Guy's lips curve up, and I can see he's struggling not to laugh.

"You're so full of shit. I saw the way you were squirming in your chair. You wanted me to fuck you in the aisle the moment you saw me." He thoughtfully muses over the memory.

"No," I say defensively. "You made me uncomfortable."

"I made your pussy uncomfortable because I wasn't inside it."

He reaches down and tickles the hairs above my clit. I laugh and squirm, tightening my legs together.

"Stop it!" I yell. "I'm still sensitive there."

Guy takes a deep breath. "I'll let you have a little rest, but I can't wait to touch you and make love to your sweet"—he kisses my shoulder—"perfect"—he kisses my left breast and rolls me further onto my back—"beautiful body."

My neck stretches up, making room for him to move under my chin where he sweetly kisses me where it's most tender.

Now, he's got me pinned, and he's staring down at me. I can't help but want to reach my hand up and touch his rough, rugged cheek. His facial hairs prick my palm as I rub my hand around to the nape of his neck and pull him down to kiss my lips.

When I allow him to pull his head back up, I ask, "Make love? I thought what we did probably resembled fucking."

He smiles a devious and sinister smile. "What's the difference? What if I love fucking you?"

*Love?* It seems twisted to hear that word.

But I suppose I have to be honest with him and say, "I love fucking you, too."

"It's more than that, Nay." His hand moves across my face, and his thumb brushes a rogue hair off my forehead.

Guy's lips move down, and I know where they're going. He's going to kiss my forehead.

*And there it is; my guilt is here to ruin this moment.*

I swiftly turn my head and avoid his lips. "I'm gonna go wash up." I make my excuse and move past his arms to sit up.

"What's wrong?" he asks.

"Nothing. I just feel like a swim; that's all."

The confusion and disappointment on his face make my heart hurt, but I can't explain why I suddenly feel uncomfortable. I can be happy here. I can be happy with Guy, but I can't shake this guilt.

"Naomi, did I do something wrong?" he asks as I stand up in front of him as he still sits on the flat boulder.

I shake my head and force a smile. "No." I reach out my hand for him to hold, and he takes it. Yanking him, trying to encourage him to stand up, I say, "Come with me. We can swim together now."

"Fucking finally," he says, trailing behind me on our way to the shallow end of the pool.

The sharp feeling of sunrays on my face makes me stir in Guy's arms. We've made an addition to our hut. We built another pallet without a roof, so we could sleep under the stars on dry nights. It's our third morning of waking up this way.

We've hardly left each other's arms since I gave in to my inner screaming to allow him to touch me. Well, there's one exception; we argued about a restaurant we had both been to in New York—Rosette. It was probably the dumbest argument in history, fighting over what their signature dish should be since everything on the menu was so good. I don't know how we got so upset with each other, but we did, and Guy somehow managed to insult me. I was so angry that we slept on different pallets—me in the interior one and him on the exterior one. He slept outside like the dog he sometimes wants to act like.

As soon as we woke, we made up quickly, and he showed me a new way to enjoy make-up sex.

Guy's muscles contract when I move against his body. I crawl up on top of him and remember last night when he was inside me while I sat, looking down on him from above. It was my first time in control and setting the pace. We came together again, but this time, I collapsed on top of him, and he hasn't let go of me until now.

His eyes painfully squint after he tries to let the morning light in. With a groggy tone and after a lengthy yawn, he says, "This scene looks oddly familiar. I could get used to waking up like this."

He grabs me and throws me to the side, off the pallet. He lands on top of me, pinning me into the warm, soft sand.

"I have to pee." I laugh. "Let me go."

"Oh no, don't tease me. You know how hard my dick gets in the morning. You can't let me wake up with you on top of me and then run off."

"Hmm," I hum with a lighthearted smirk. "How can I forget?"

While straddling me, he takes my arms and moves them together above my head. "Oh, you are a little tease. I'm gonna have to teach you a lesson."

"How about this?" I say with my sultriest tone. "Why don't you let me go pee? Then, I'll be back, and we can put each other out of our misery." I reach my head up as far and as best I can while my hands are still pinned behind my head and lift my lips to kiss his sweet-tasting mouth.

Guy lets go of my hand, and I roll over onto all fours. Before I can attempt to stand up, he smacks an exciting, tingling slap on my ass.

"You'd better hurry," he says as I get to my feet and head off into the island's wilderness.

After I go to the bathroom, I remember to mark another day in the calendar on my way back to Guy. I pick up the rock and pause for a moment.

*Why am I still doing this? If another day goes by, does it really matter?*

I count the tallies. My eyes move across the groups of four straight lines and one diagonal line slashed across them. *Five, ten, fifteen, twenty, twenty-five, thirty, and one more mark makes another group of five.*

We've been here for thirty-five days, plus the three when we were on the raft. Feels more like a lifetime than thirty-eight days.

*Wait.* I look down to my abdomen. I still haven't gotten my period. I might really be pregnant. I can't deny it anymore. I think I really am pregnant. For sure, I would have gotten my period by now.

I cautiously walk out onto the sunlit beach. Guy senses me coming up behind him.

"Finally. I was about to send a search party," he says while turning around but freezes when he sees the look on my face. "Naomi, what is it? What happened?" He darts over to me in two steps and puts his hands on my shoulders. "Are you okay?"

I swallow slow and hard, pushing down the nervousness running through me. This really complicates things. Our lives will be so much harder, surviving here with a baby. *Am I really going to have to give natural birth on an island, away from a hospital?* I never thought I'd have to consider that when Charles and I first decided to try to get pregnant.

"It's just that I realized I still haven't gotten my period," I nervously tell him.

Guy takes a step back and moves his eyes to my middle. "So, you think you're definitely pregnant?"

I nod slowly. "I think so." It's the only thing that makes sense with the facts we have.

His brows move down, and his eyes squint, focusing on my stomach. "But you haven't gotten any bigger."

I roll my eyes. "Well, it's the first time I've been pregnant. It might take a little longer before I start showing. Plus, I'm not exactly eating for two *here.*"

He considers my words and nods. "We'll have to change that."

"You're not worried?" I ask, wanting to get the honest truth out of him. "Because I'm terrified."

He brushes my tangled and knotted hair behind my shoulders on each side. His fingers rise up from my nape, and he cups the back of my head.

His lips look so full and luscious. They have no comparison to the softness and current kindness he holds in his eyes.

"Naomi, I love you. I love every tiny thing inside you, and I would rather die than let anything happen to you or your baby. The only thing I'm afraid of is losing you."

His words are like an emotional song playing in my head. Those soft, tempting lips draw me in, and I get to taste the side of Guy I like most—his sensual and sweet side. I let him kiss me senseless … until …

My eyes pop open, and my face pulls away from him. "Wait. What is that? Do you see that?"

# Twenty-One

My hand goes up and points to a little black blip in the sky.

"I do." Guy places one hand above his brows, blocking the sun. "It's pretty far off. Do you want to try to send up a smoke signal?"

"What's the point?" I mumble to myself.

I put a smile on my face and turn my head back to Guy. "No. I think you're right. It's too far."

His hand slides down my back and soothes my spine, rubbing in a circular motion. "Are you sure you don't want to try?"

I keep my light smile and shake my head. "We've seen dozens of planes in the far distance. They've never come this way."

I stare into his eyes and get lost in them for a moment. I can hardly remember what we were talking about. He seems equally tranced, staring back at me.

Forgetting about the plane in the distance, all I want closer to me right now are Guy's lips. And he knows it.

He draws near until we're touching, and it's like an explosion ignites inside us. Just the mere gentle touch of his lips on mine is enough to set off a chain reaction of excitement, reaching all the way down to my toes.

I've never felt so free, so weightless, than I do in his arms.

Something takes over me, and I need to have a taste of Guy's skin. "You're all I need right now," I say in his ear before nibbling on it. Feeling any part of his skin in my mouth is erotic.

He lets out a gentle moan and pulls his head away, taking both hands and placing one on each side of my face. "You're all I'll ever need."

It's as if we were the only two people in the world. We *are* the only two people in our own little world.

Throughout the week, the morning sun has gotten harsher each day. I can even feel its intensity through the roof of our hut where the wood isn't completely flush or even with the branches next to it.

We both look up when a sharp sting of light crawls across our eyes.

My hand lies gently on his chest, running my fingers through his hairs—one of my favorite textures and things to touch.

With squinting eyes, Guy says, "I think I should create a second layer on the roof to prevent leaks, and then I can put a layer of banana leaves between them to block out any light."

"Ah, blackout shades," I say with delight, moving my hand further down his abdomen. I lightly trail my fingers over his belly button and past the deep pockets created by his pelvis, giving me a direct path to his most virile body part.

He looks down with eager eyes, watching my hand move over his semi-erect cock. My fingers gently curve around, and I can feel it stiffen.

I curiously look at it. "I want …" But then I chicken out and don't finish my sentence.

"What, baby? What do you want?" The anticipation makes him breathe harder.

I glance at him. He's giving me an encouraging look, wanting me to finish my thought.

"I want to know what it's like to feel it as it gets hard."

He gives me a strange look and says, "Well, I'm not going to argue." But still, there's skepticism in his voice.

I shake my head, keeping my fingers over his shaft. "I know it sounds crazy. I know what a hard penis looks and feels like. It's just … I've never actually felt it as it got to that point. Knowing I'm the one driving its reaction."

Guy's breath is shallow and heavy. "Oh, you're the one driving it all right." There's a hunger in his eyes that tells me to keep going.

Looking back down at his beautiful cock below me, I tighten my grip around his girth and feel it twitch, filling with more life. My hand moves up and down while my fingers stay curved around it. But not too tight because I can feel it growing, testing my grip. It doesn't take long for it to become fully erect and thriving, craving more stimulation. My mouth waters as I look at it.

I've never felt this way. I've never had this drive or desire inside me to put my mouth on anyone's body. But looking down at Guy's hard cock gives me the urge to wrap my lips around it. There's something about his scent and taste that drives my insides crazy. And, now, my insides want to taste what's in my hand.

I look at him, and it's almost as if he's reading my mind.

"Now, are you going to tell me," he says breathlessly, "that you've never given a blow job?"

I shrug innocently and can't help but grin. Exploring each other was just never part of my and Charles's marriage. I've never had the desire to explore anyone sexually … until now.

Guy gives me a nod, telling me to use him as I please.

I look into his eyes as I lower down. He sits up on his elbows to maintain eye contact as long as possible until my lips hit the tip of his penis. His head falls back, and he lets out an audible breath. I've hardly touched him, and I feel like I have complete control over his body.

My tongue slowly darts out and licks the rim around the head. And, now, I know exactly what I want to do. I put my whole mouth over the top and move down over his thick girth, moving my hand under my mouth.

I had no idea my instincts could drive me to do something like this.

I pump my mouth up and down, sucking in as I move, wanting to taste as much of his salty flesh as possible.

"Naomi," he cries out, reaching down and running his fingers through my hair on top of my head. "Oh, baby, you make me so hard."

I love the reaction I'm giving him. I love how my mouth is bringing as much of him inside me as possible. A throbbing pulse begins between my legs. It makes me feel ravenous.

I begin moving up and down over him faster and sucking harder.

"Baby, slow down," he groans. "You're gonna make me come."

It's as if that's a trigger for me. I can't stop. Not now that I've elicited this power I have over him.

"Oh no," Guy says, sitting up straighter. "You've had enough fun. It's my turn now."

He reaches down, grabbing me under my armpits, and pulls me up to him. He rolls us over until he's on top of me.

His expression is intense, and he looks as if he wants to devour me. He bends his head down to my neck and opens his mouth, as if to take a bite. But he exercises control, only scraping my skin with his teeth.

"The only place I want to come in this morning," he whispers over my mouth as he places his thumb inside my sex, "is here."

"Oh," I breathe out at the thought. Now that he's said that, I want nothing else.

I squirm and move my hips up closer to his hard dick, which is lying right between my legs but not going where I want it yet.

I'm wet and pulsing, and I need him now.

"Guy," I plead.

He knows exactly what I want.

His lips dive into me, and he kisses me hard. I instinctively pull my knees up, making me open and so, so ready for him. He grabs ahold of himself and shoves his cock right into me.

It goes in fast and hard but immediately slows down as he pulls back.

It's as if a void I was missing all my life has been filled. I'm sore from the past several days of constant sex, but it's a feeling of belonging. Like he's supposed to be inside me, and we were made to do this with each other.

He keeps moving at a steady pace. My hips move along with him, meeting him at my deepest spot. A sound escapes me every time we hit that tender and barely reachable place inside me. It's been untouched until Guy.

Our breaths mingle between us as we stare into each other's eyes. There's this force we've created whenever we're together.

There's a twitch I see under his eyes as he speeds up, and I know he's getting closer, drawing me closer with him every time he hits my back wall. It's a need that gets filled and builds with every movement.

My fingers claw into his shoulder blades, as I'm trying to have some sort of power over the intensity that's growing, and I wonder if I can control anything that's happening inside my body. He knows I'm about to come undone.

His voice is gruff as he says, "Naomi," keeping his eyes bored into me.

"Guy," I answer in return.

My name coming out of his mouth and me saying his is like we're claiming each other, and it is enough to put us both over the edge.

I cry out while he grunts, convulsing on top of me as my insides melt and ooze into every nerve in my body.

It takes us a while to calm our breaths and feel our muscles come back to life. Guy slowly pulls out of me, rolling to his side, scooping his arm under the back of my shoulders. He pulls me in close, and I curl into his naked body.

"Are you happy?" he asks, kissing my head.

"Mmhmm," I answer in a hum.

How could I be anything but? I'm completely sated.

I smile, closing my eyes and breathing the scent of Guy's skin under my nose. My body feels so relaxed; I could almost drift back to sleep.

*Chhh-chhh-chhh.*

The sound reminds me of a faraway washing machine. I listen, letting it soothe me for a few seconds.

"Nay." Guy's arm flinches under me.

*Chhh-chhh-chhh.*

The sound continues.

"I hear it, too. I'm sure it's too far away."

"Yeah, but …" Guy sits up, forcing me to sit up with him.

I'm almost afraid to get my hopes up. *It can't be*, I tell myself, knowing this would be too good to be true.

*Chhh-chhh-chhh-chhh.*

"It's getting louder." He jumps to his feet. He bends down, grabbing what's left of his tattered clothes and putting them on. "I'd better go check it out."

# Twenty-Two

"Here!" I scream, waving my arms up and down. "We're here!" I turn and look at Guy, who seems as stunned as I feel. "Am I crazy, or is that helicopter coming straight toward us?"

Looking as if he's in a state of shock, Guy says, "Nay, you're not crazy. It's low, too. Shit, Nay, I think they know we're here."

I scream out loud, putting all my efforts to be heard into the air around me.

*I can't believe this is actually happening!*

There's no mistaking this. We've been spotted, and the helicopter is coming to get us. I scream and jump into Guy's arms. He sets me down and yells, flexing every muscle in his body.

The helicopter is nearly at our island. Sand starts to blow in every direction, forcing Guy and me to shield our eyes. But my smile doesn't leave my face. My overwhelming excitement couldn't possibly die down.

There's a brief calm in the air as the aircraft takes a short lap above the small island, coming back to hover over us.

"Guy Harrington and Naomi Devereux?"

We jump up and wave our arms, nodding.

"We're here to rescue you!" A stranger's voice blares over a loudspeaker coming from the chopper. "Are there any other survivors?"

Guy and I both wildly shake our heads back and forth.

"Stay where you are. We'll circle around and see if there's a place to land. If not, we'll be back with a rescue basket, and we'll get you home."

The helicopter turns in the air and flies back the way it came.

I spin around in a gleeful circle and scream, "We're saved! We're saved!" I run and jump into Guy's arms. I wrap my legs around him and begin to cry happy tears.

I pull my head back before looking at his face. He's just as happy as I am, and I kiss his lips, wanting to celebrate this incredible breakthrough with him.

But then it hits.

*Oh no.*

My legs come down, but I don't move my body. I keep holding on to him tightly, as if I might lose him if I let go. Saying nothing, Guy strokes my hair, and I cry into his shoulder as if he's comforting me. He holds me so close, and I embrace him back.

I push back to look at Guy, wanting to see the expression on his face. I'm wondering if he has the same realization as I do. And I can see he does—or at least, he knows what I'm thinking.

"Oh no … Charles," I say barely louder than a whisper. "What have I done?"

His arm reaches around, cupping my shoulder blades, and suddenly, his touch feels wrong and offensive. I squirm.

"Nay, don't." He scolds me with his eyes. "It's going to be fine."

I walk backward, away from him. "For who?" I ask.

"For us," he says, defending himself. "We're adults. I can see the look on your face, and you don't have to be ashamed of anything. You don't have to be ashamed of *me*"—his hand goes close to his body—"and what we have."

I begin to cry. In a moment when my only tears should be of pure joy and relief, I'm crying because I'm ashamed of myself.

"We're rescued!" he yells, waving his arm up in the air. "We can go home now. Doesn't that make you fucking happy?"

"There's no *we*," I snap quickly.

He slaps his arms down to his sides. "Can't you just be happy, and we'll deal with the rest later? Why do you always have to make everything so complicated?"

"Because it *is* complicated. It's complicated now that I've been with you, and I have to explain that to my husband!"

He stands his ground and raises his voice. "You're an adult, Naomi! You can own up to what we've done. You don't have to be ashamed of it. What we have is fucking great!" he screams.

Something solid turns in my stomach. It's a churning of dread. But, when the sound of the helicopter blades fills the air again, my stomach jolts with fuzzy anticipation. Confusing and conflicting emotions swirl around inside me.

"Was," I utter out, correcting him. But I'm not even sure he can hear me anymore.

Once the helicopter comes back and hovers above us again, they send down a large wire basket and instruct us to get in one at a time and allow them to draw us back up to the helicopter. The beach is too narrow for them to land anywhere on the island.

With Guy holding my hips, I hold on to the suspending ropes and lift my foot up to place it at the end of the basket, but my insides pull me back.

"No." I shake my head. "I can't do this. You have to go first. I can't do this."

His hands still on my hips. He pulls me down and lets my feet fall back to the sand. He turns me to face him and places his hands on my shoulders. "If I know anything about you, there's nothing you're not capable of. You can do *this*, Nay. I'm not taking one foot off this island until I know you're safe first." Cupping my cheeks, he whispers, "I know being rescued means you're leaving me. Let me help you this one last time."

His eyes cry to me, and mine fill with tears again. This is such an overwhelming moment. I suck up my strength and nod, allowing myself to give him this last opportunity to protect me and put me first.

For a short time, I might have thought I belonged to him. But I was wrong. I belong to Charles, and there's nothing either Guy or I can do about that.

"Okay," I agree. "But I know you're right behind me. I can't be on that helicopter without you. I can't be in the air unless I know you'll be with me."

His lips barely brush the tip of my nose. I look up, and our mouths are almost touching. This rescue has been so abrupt. I have this urge to give him a good-bye kiss. Or take him to the hut and have a long conversation about how we're going to move forward—or not move forward. But I gather my strength, take a deep breath, and lean my body further away from him.

One nod, and I know we are on the same page. It's time to move on and go back to where we belong.

I turn back toward the basket and allow him to help me in. He tightens the straps across my lap, giving me one long look of desperation, and then he steps back to give the pilots a thumbs-up.

*This is how I'm leaving the island.*

Just me, hoisted up, alone. There's only room for one of us to go up at a time. And it feels really empty.

The moments until he joins me are agony, but then I think about the impending reunion I'll finally have with my husband. I'm torn between the two longings.

Fifteen minutes later, Guy is safe and secure in the helicopter with me. We sit on the floor—me wedged between Guy and the rescuer who helped me out of the basket and into the helicopter. I feel more secure in the middle than I would near the doorless sides.

I tighten the blanket the copilot gave me around my whole body with only my feet sticking out. I lean my head back and close my eyes, trying to imagine solid ground again. Guy lets his hand fall to the floor and inches it over to my ankle. Out of sight from the pilots and the other rescuer on board, he wraps his fingers around me and holds my foot more firmly to the floor, giving me an added boost of stability.

"Do either of you need immediate medical attention?" the rescuer at my side shouts over the loud sound of the helicopter blades above us.

Guy snaps up, leaning forward to have a better vantage point to answer him. "Yes!" he shouts. "She thinks she might—"

"No!" I yell, giving Guy a pleading look.

I can't discuss this pregnancy without Charles. He needs to know and be a part of it before anyone else. Guy gives me a warning look, and I subtly shake my head at him.

"He"—I point my finger at Guy—"was attacked. His leg. It was a jellyfish."

Guy's lips tense as they tighten together.

"Let me take a look," the rescuer says, bending across me, wondering which leg on Guy is the injured one.

"Here." Guy bends his right leg and pulls his loose pant leg up, revealing the scars and the larger wound that's still healing.

"We think it was infected!" I shout while the rescuer closely examines it without touching. "That one opened up and had pus," I say, pointing at it. "He was sick and had a fever for a few days."

The rescuer nods, saving his breath.

"It's fine now!" Guy pushes his pant leg down and straightens his leg, away from the rescuer.

The rescuer takes the hint and sits back.

"You're still limping. I can see it!" I snap at Guy.

"It hasn't stopped me from *doing* anything that needed to be done," he loudly seethes.

But I don't think anyone but me can hear him.

I inhale an angry breath and look away from Guy.

*Stubborn ass*, I think to myself.

But, after a few moments of only the sounds of the helicopter, I'm craving some sort of interaction with him. I bite the inside of my lower lip and fight the urge to move my fingers closer to his hand.

"Where are we going?" Guy asks, straining his voice to be heard.

The pilot tilts his head in Guy's direction. "Aircraft carrier," he explains. "Only a few more miles."

"Where are we?" Guy yells to him again.

His head tilts back the same way. "About one hundred fifty miles off the coast of Bermuda."

Guy slams his back down to a resting position. He turns to me and says, barely audible but I can hear his murmurs through the noise, "Bermuda. Why couldn't we have washed up there? You could have found your five-star resort."

I try to force a smile but otherwise remain motionless and wordless for the rest of the ride.

"Where is my husband?" I shout at a man in uniform, who's greeting us, as Guy holds my hand to help me out of the helicopter.

"Mrs. Devereux." He extends his hand for me to shake. "Welcome back. I'm Major Chan."

I ignore his hand and repeat, "Where's my husband?" This time, my words hold more desperation.

He allows his hand to fall down to his side without any signs of being insulted. "He wanted to meet us here when we sent word that you'd been found, but we can't allow or afford civilian transportation to an aircraft carrier. You and Mr.

Harrington will be flown to New York, and you will meet up with your spouses there."

*Spouses.* The word rings in my head.

I don't just have Charles to feel guilty over. They're not divorced. I've betrayed Guy's wife. I've become someone I despise.

The major clears his throat before continuing, "You'll need to be debriefed and interviewed after you are checked out by a doctor."

"No," I quickly retort. "I will do that in New York."

Guy interjects before Major Chan has a chance to argue with my demand, "Naomi, I think it's smart to see a doctor." He turns to face the major. "But then we can be debriefed in the city, right?"

"No." I raise my voice, controlling both men's attention. "I am not doing anything." I look at Guy. "Not even seeing a doctor." I turn to Major Chan. "Not talking to anyone until I'm back in New York."

The major's jaw tightens, and Guy's nose sneers the way it does when he's annoyed with me, but he keeps his lips tight until the major caves.

"All right, Mrs. Devereux." Disapproval spreads across his face. He looks to Guy. "As long as Mr. Harrington agrees to give his testimony of what happened, we can work everything else out in New York."

Guy nods reluctantly. "Give the lady what she wants."

A little spin of victory courses through me. It accompanies my anxiousness and anticipation to see my husband, my best friend since college.

But, before I can walk off and follow Major Chan, Guy grabs my arm, tugging me back closer to him. "But you'd better see a doctor." His hand subtly glides across and grazes my abdomen.

I know where his hand is and what he's trying to say, but my body is screaming in reaction to his skin being near my body.

I look down to where he touched me. "Of course," I whisper back to him.

It just wouldn't be right if this pregnancy were addressed any further without Charles being involved.

As much as I crave Guy's touch, I'm supposed to be with my husband.

# Twenty-Three

The Coast Guard sweatpants and sweatshirt Major Chan gave me are baggy, but they fit enough for me to wear home. They offered food, but I'm not ready to eat yet. I'm afraid of what it will feel like. I need to make sure I'm not in an emotional state so that I can take it in slowly.

I must have taken almost an hour in the shower. There was dirt in more places than I'd care to admit. A shower was necessary. Finally, I feel clean again. But there's no amount of soap that could wash the feel of Guy's body against mine. He's still weighing on my mind.

Coming out of the room they let me shower and change in, I bump into someone. And, before looking up, I already know who it is. I melt into him and rest my head on his chest.

"Guy?" My voice is muffled in his sweatshirt.

His hand rubs my back, soothing me. "Yeah?" he answers.

I push back to look at him. "I'm married."

"I know," he says, looking so serious. He continues to rub my back in a circular motion. "Technically, so am I. But we can figure this all out when we get back."

I take another step back and shake my head.

"Nay," he warns, stepping toward me.

I back up again. "No!" I stop him, holding my hands up. "This might be the last time we're alone, and I need to say this."

"Naomi, you can't be serious," he spits out.

"I am serious," I say, raising my trembling voice. "This was a mistake, and it never should have happened. When we get back to New York, I don't want to see you. *I can't.*"

He exhales, clearly frustrated, and puts his hands on his hips. "Look," he says, trying to stay calm, "you're emotional. We've been through a lot, and we've just been rescued. I'm sure there's a lot going through your mind, but you can't just throw what we have away."

I take a few more steps backward, still facing him, and say, "What we have? We never should have had it in the first place. I'm going back to New York and leaving everything we did in the past and on that island."

Then, I turn and walk away, convincing myself I'm doing the right thing.

*I am doing the right thing.*

Two members of the National Transportation Safety Board (NTSB) ride with us in a medium-sized military plane. There are ten passengers total. Five sit on each side of the inner shell of the plane, facing the center. The belly of this plane was built to carry cargo or a large handful of people. It's louder than the private jet we were on that fell out of the sky, but it's quieter than the helicopter I was in less than an hour ago.

"I'm sorry," I sheepishly say to the female passenger with the NTSB badge on her navy-blue windbreaker.

She leans forward and gives me an empathetic smile.

"Ma'am, I understand. But we really need to get your statements while the information is as fresh in your mind as possible."

My lips tighten, so I don't reveal anything. I'm not saying a word until I'm back where I belong. She understands and leans back in her seat.

Guy is sitting in the seat directly next to me. His fingers are intertwined together on his lap, his ankle sitting on the knee of his other leg. He's just staring straight forward, similar to the moment I first met him. He's brooding, and I know it's because of what I said to him.

His fingers unfold, and his hand falls to the side of his thigh. My hand is on top of my own thigh, and my pinkie finger is hanging on the side. Without looking, Guy moves his fingers closer to my pinkie. He brushes it, and I don't move, paralyzed with uncertainty. He moves again, attempting to hook one of his fingers around my pinkie, but then decisiveness hits me, and I quickly move it away.

We're not on the island anymore. I just can't allow myself to feel this way.

Guy's expression remains dormant, and he's still looking ahead. I wonder what he's thinking, but then I realize I don't want to know what he's thinking. I only want him to keep his thoughts off of me.

He opens his mouth to speak, and I worry that he'll try to have a private conversation when others are around. But his eyes pass me and go to the NTSB woman.

"Why did the plane's engines fail?" he simply asks.

She leans forward, giving him more of her attention. "We suspect we know the cause, but we can't confirm until we have your statement. Once we hear your testimony of the event, we'll let you know what conclusion we come to."

Guy nods, disappointed there aren't more answers yet.

It is a quick forty-five-minute flight. This plane travels much faster than a civilian jet or commercial aircraft. As soon as the wheels hit the ground, I play at my safety belt, but Guy's arm reaches across and stills my movements.

"Not yet," he warns.

Once I get out, I hope my feet never step foot in another airplane again.

*That was my last ride*, I think to myself as the plane comes to a rolling stop, *in more ways than one.*

I look to Guy for quick reassurance. He nods, and then I hastily tear at my safety belt to spring me loose. I stand up at the same time the pilot reappears from the cockpit. He works at the door for a moment, but then it pops open and lifts out of the way.

There's a big gaping hole almost ten feet off the ground. With no windows in the belly where we sat, this is my first glimpse of being back in New York. It's my first opportunity to look for my husband's tall, lanky body, charming bald head, and comforting face.

I see him in the distance, gathered with a group of about twenty people. He's taking a step toward our plane, but a man in uniform places his hand on Charles's chest. Charles easily calms, but his eyes remain locked on the plane. I want to leap to him, and my body acts accordingly. My hand reaches out to shove the pilot out of my way, but Guy holds me around my waist with both hands.

"Not yet," he tells me again in my ear.

His voice soothes me, and my body calms. I lean back into him, letting him hold me until it's clear for me to get off this plane.

His lips stay close to my ear. "Whatever happens, you need to know that you're always going to be the only woman in the world to me."

I grab on to his hand that's wrapped around me. I feel passion between us, but it's confusing with the adrenaline I feel for seeing my husband at the same time.

I consider turning around and telling Guy that there's a part of me that will always see him as the only man in the world, too.

*There's no decision*, I tell myself.

Guy has no place in my life here. The part of me that feels this strongly toward Guy is back on the island, and I have to leave it all behind.

I shove his hands off me, making a statement.

Once the rolling staircase reaches the open doorway, the pilot steps out of the way and allows me to pass. I run down the steps, yelling for Charles, and he impulsively does the same. He moves right past the guard who is placed there to contain where the crowd moves. He doesn't seem to mind when Charles forces himself right past him. He just turns his head and smiles as Charles runs to me.

Our bodies crash into each other, and everything I've been holding in since I knew I would see him and feel his familiarity again comes crashing in, too. I sob wildly in his arms. I've been so scared, so uncertain, tried and tested emotionally and physically, and now, it's all over. My emotions don't know how to handle it.

Charles cries along with me. Neither of us is able to speak a word. I nuzzle my head to the side on his shoulder as if it were my pillow. His cashmere sweater soaks up my tears.

I can feel Guy walking past us. He's only a few feet ahead of the two people from NTSB. His exit from the plane was much less rushed than mine, and I don't have the capacity to even wonder why. He looks down on us, and our eyes meet when he passes by.

The woman from the plane looks at Guy and me, back and forth, as she continues to pass by as well. My stomach turns at the thought that she knows what we did, but I try to put that far in the back of my mind and tell myself she's just waiting to speak to the both of us. I know she wants to talk to me, but I don't want her to approach me now. I need a moment to reunite with my husband.

My stare at Guy holds until we both hear a woman screaming his name.

"Guy! Guy, baby, you're okay!" she yells.

I pick my head up from Charles's shoulder and straighten to get a better look.

She's beautiful, and her legs aren't just long; they're sculpted poles. Her whole body is perfectly shaped and proportioned at every inch and corner. Her face is pristine, and her pouty lips could make every man, woman, child, or animal want to kiss them.

Guy doesn't return her calls, but he opens his arms as she throws her body onto him. She madly kisses him. If his face wasn't so expressionless, I'd have to guess that he was annoyed. Not the same kind of annoyed he gets with me where his nose scrunches. His expression is more about disinterest.

"Marina, that's enough," Guy says.

A man steps out from the group of people who have gathered and takes a photo of them. The paparazzi must have followed her here. I imagine the paparazzi follow her everywhere.

"Baby, things are going to be different now," she immediately responds to him.

"I can't believe it's you." Charles's voice brings me back to him.

I sniffle and try to force a smile in his direction.

"You're so skinny," he says with his arms wrapped easily around my entire body.

We both muster a laugh. I nod, knowing what he must think of my dwindled frame. He turns, guiding me closer to the large crowd, still cradling me in the wing of his arm.

"We need to get you some food," he says, walking with such a concerned hold on me.

"Yes, I think I'm ready for that now."

Before we reach the automatic sliding glass doors that stand as the entrance to the military airport, he turns me to face him. "What would you like, my darling? Name anything."

I think about that. I think about what I really want, what I've been craving this whole time I've been gone. "I want you to take me home, and I want … I really, really want a classic pie from Rubirosa."

Charles breathes in a thoughtful and clear breath and runs the pad of his thumb over my forehead. I close my eyes, savoring the familiarity, and wait to feel the touch of his tender kiss. It feels as safe and serene as it always has.

We continue to walk a few more feet where more friends and family have been waiting patiently to greet me back home.

"Naomi," Samantha says between tears, opening her arms up to me.

She has been my best friend since elementary school. We grew up next door to each other. There might have been a few acres separating our houses, but we were like two peas in a pod, growing up.

I hug her and try not to cry more on her shoulder. I'm eager to see everyone, but I'm more eager to go home. I just want to go back to where I belong.

Over Samantha's shoulder, I see one of the kindest, most genuine, and classiest women I've ever known.

"Mama," I call out to her and leave Samantha for the comfort of my mother's arms.

"Oh, my darling girl." She sobs in my embrace.

We take a moment for just us before I leave her to hug my father.

Charles follows me close behind as I hug and greet my loved ones.

"Ma'am." The woman on the plane from NTSB taps me on the shoulder.

Charles puts his arm around me as I turn to her.

"I'm sorry to interrupt, Mrs. Devereux, but we really need to take your statement now."

"I was just about to take my wife home, miss. Can't this wait until later? You can come to our home and interview her tomorrow if you'd like," Charles says with a naivety to the importance of her job.

She gives him an insincere smile.

"Actually, honey"—I turn and place my hands on Charles's chest—"I promised her I would give my statement as soon as we were in New York."

"My partner is interviewing Mr. Harrington now. Timing *is* important here. We would also like to take you up on your offer and have a follow-up interview tomorrow morning after you've rested. There will be more questions after we get answers."

"She needs to eat," Charles protectively says.

"It's fine." I smile reassuringly to him. "I'll have a snack while they ask their questions. I still want that whole pie when we get home."

My promise to eat is enough to settle him into supporting me from staying away from our penthouse a little longer. I think he wants me to get home and to comfort me as much as I do.

I gave my statement in a private room at the military airport we landed at, just outside of Manhattan. Charles waited patiently outside while he assured Samantha and my family that he would take care of me for the night and that they could see me tomorrow.

After the questioning, Charles ushers me to the town car he has waiting. I'm physically and emotionally exhausted. But I can't seem to settle my mind. There are too many thoughts flying around—mostly about Guy. I shake my head, needing to think about something else.

"What happened with the schools?" I ask Charles. "Was there a strike? *Is* there a strike?" I correct myself.

"No, darling," he speaks in a soothing tone. "There hasn't been a strike. It's all been taken care of. Don't worry about a thing. Take as much time as you need to recover before going back to your work."

I breathe in a deep sigh of relief.

# Twenty-Four

Charles kept his promise and had a whole classic pie from Rubirosa delivered to our home. In fact, he had two sent up. Our housekeeper informed him that the first one was delivered ten minutes ahead of schedule, and since we were a few minutes behind, he asked her to order a new one so that it was as fresh and warm as possible. He knew I didn't enjoy reheated pizza. But, honestly, I'd have eaten just about anything at that point. Hot, cold—it didn't matter as long as it wasn't a banana.

I devoured that pizza. After one bite, I became ravenous for every crumb. Unfortunately, I became sick not long after I finished it.

I decided not to tell Charles about the baby last night. I was too emotionally and physically exhausted. All I wanted to do was take a bath and sleep.

When Charles was lying with me, I went to move my hand under his shirt to feel his chest hairs, but he startled.

"What are you doing?" he asked.

"I just want to touch you."

He squirmed but let me continue. My fingers moved around. I hoped I'd get the same sensation when I had done this with Guy. But it was different. I didn't feel much when I did it.

It must be this guilt I have that's keeping me from feeling like myself with my husband. I can't go on with lying to him. I need to tell him what I did with Guy and pray to God that he forgives me.

"Honey," I call to him from the living room sofa as he walks in with a tray, carrying coffee, toast, and an omelet our live-in housekeeper put together.

He sets the tray down on the large ottoman in front of me, and I pat the seat to my left, asking him to join me on the sofa. Charles moves in and slides his arm across my back, pulling me into leaning against him.

I take a deep breath, savoring the comforting and familiar smell of home. I love this scent. We have remodeled and decorated twice since we've lived here in this prewar penthouse, but for some mysterious reason, it still smells of deep mahogany and antiques.

I'm in my silk robe and fresh out of my second bath since I've been home. Charles has been attending to my every move for the past eighteen hours. He opened the terrace doors, so I could have more fresh air. I'm surprised how warm it is. I feel as if I was gone so long that it should be at least the middle of winter, but we're just getting into the middle of summer. Each day stranded felt like an eternity.

"Darling, you'd better eat your breakfast and get dressed. The investigators from the NTSB will be here in a little more than thirty minutes."

"I know," I lazily say and then tilt my head up to look at Charles's sweet, genuine face. "I love you," I whisper, searching his eyes and hoping to see a fiery passion staring back at me. But I just see warmth and contentment.

"I love you, too," he replies with all his tenderness and moves his thumb over my forehead before kissing me there.

I need to tell him what happened. I'm terrified of hurting him, but I can't live with myself if I keep my infidelity a secret from him. He deserves so much more.

I try to speak, but my chin quivers. "Charles, I-I—"

But he interrupts me before I can form a real word, "Darling, please eat your breakfast."

He's right. I do need to eat. I plan on eating much slower this morning, and hopefully, I won't get sick again.

"You're right. But then I really need to talk to you."

"Of course, honey." He rubs my back after I sit up to eat my food. "You've been through so much."

I slowly savor each bite, but I still clean my plate. Charles takes the empty tray of food and stands up to bring it into the kitchen. I follow him in.

"After she made your breakfast, I asked Kathy to take the rest of the day off so that we could have privacy and let you relax," he explains.

I nod. "I think that's a good idea." My guilt is eating away at me, and I feel as if I need to get my secret off my chest.

After unloading the tray into the sink and dishwasher, he rounds the kitchen island to where I am and wraps his arms around me. "Oh, Naomi, I can't believe I finally have you back," he says. "All those weeks without you felt like a lifetime."

"I know exactly what you mean. It felt like a lifetime for me, too." I clear my throat and begin to form the words in my mind before letting them hit the air. "Charles, I have to tell you something."

"I was losing my mind, not knowing what had happened to you, but I knew you were still out there," he says without thought to what I'm trying to tell him. His eyebrows rise, as if he just had a brilliant idea. "Wait right here. There's something I want to show you."

He releases me and turns to walk down the long hallway that leads to the study at the far corner of the west wing of our penthouse.

Once his frame is out of sight, the doorbell chimes.

I look down at my thin cream-colored robe. Kathy is likely in her quarters and not minding the front door since she has the day off. The bell doesn't reach the study where

Charles darted off to, and it would be rude to leave someone at our doorstep while I change into more appropriate clothes.

*Damn, I'll just have to answer in my robe.*

I'm sure it's the investigators. I can excuse myself as soon as I let them in.

I tighten the lapels with one overlapping the other as much as possible and tie the silk belt into a knot, securing my robe closed. The doorman wouldn't allow anyone who wasn't on the list up, so I'm not in the practice of checking the peephole before opening. I crack the door first and peer through, covering the rest of my body.

For a moment, my heart skips a beat. But I remind myself where I am, who he is, and how wrong I have been.

He looks as handsome and clean-shaven as the moment I met him. I almost forgot how gorgeous and masculine his strong jawline looked without all the hair covering it up.

"What are you doing here?" I ask, feeling like I'm about to panic. I pull my robe across my body even further, testing the limits of the fabric, and fold my arms over myself.

Guy's eyes shift up and down my body. I can see a hunger ignite inside him.

"You need to leave," I quickly say and reach my hand outside the doorway to push him back before narrowing the door's opening.

I intend to shut it all the way and pretend as if he never showed up at my husband's and my home, but Guy places his hand out, making it impossible for me to close the door.

"Would you stop it?" I seethe. "You need to leave now."

"No, I don't," he grunts and forces the door open wide enough for him to step past me. He looks up and all around the foyer. "Beautiful architecture."

I ignore his compliment, letting go of the door and allowing him to close it behind himself.

My fingers fidget with my robe again before I fold my arms back over my chest. "This is not a good time. Can you please leave?"

"No, I can't," he simply says and takes a few steps further into my home.

I step in front of him and place my flat palm on his chest. "Please, Guy, you can't be here," I whisper up to him, begging.

His hand slowly comes up to meet mine on his chest. He places his over mine and rubs his thumb over my knuckles, igniting sparks in its wake.

My chest feels heavy, and time seems to stop. We breathe in unison, looking into each other's eyes.

"Actually, Nay—" he starts to say.

"Oh, hello." Charles's voice travels from down the hallway.

Guy and I both drop our hands, and I go back to pointlessly retightening my robe across my body. Charles's long strides bring him into the foyer to quickly join us.

"Honey," I nervously begin to say, "this is G—"

"Guy Harrington." Charles extends his hand out to Guy.

Without hesitation, Guy meets him halfway, and they shake.

I feel sick, watching them interact with each other. I might actually be sick. My stomach turns, and acid creeps up into my throat. I hold it there, keeping my nausea at bay as best I can.

Charles moves to place his arm around me. "Darling, why don't you go get dressed? I shouldn't have left you to attend the door before you had a chance to change. I'll show Mr. Harrington in until you're ready."

My husband has his eyes on me, but I look past them and see Guy's reaction. He's moving his brows up and down at the mention of me in my robe. The hunger returns to his eyes. He seems to be enjoying this moment while I'm feeling terrified.

I swallow nervously. "Of course. But I think Mr. Harrington was just stopping by to see how we were doing, and he'll be leaving now."

"Mrs. Devereux, please call me Guy," he says sternly, making this moment very awkward.

I scold him with my eyes and then quickly try to plead with him. I hope he gets the message and just goes.

"Oh, honey. I'm so sorry I neglected to mention it. Mr. Harrington is here for the interview. When they requested a joint follow-up interview with the two of you, I insisted they do it at our home, so you could be comfortable. Mr. Harrington was nice enough to oblige."

"It's no problem," Guy smugly says.

I begin to back away, knowing I cannot get myself out of this. "I see. Well, I'll just go change then. The investigators will be here soon."

Both men watch me move down the hall. One unsuspecting and the other looking very devious.

It doesn't take long for the investigators to arrive, and it's the same two people. After I bring some refreshments, we sit in the living room and talk. The questions are innocent enough and easy to answer with the knowledge we have, but being in the same room with Guy and my husband makes me very uneasy.

Charles sits with me on the couch while I explain the noise I heard when I was in the airplane restroom and how things seemed to really go crazy after that. Guy jumps in and tells them what the pilot said over the loudspeaker.

Talking about the crash makes me feel anxious. After I shift to a more comfortable position, Charles places his hand on my thigh. Guy's eyes hone in on my leg where my husband's hand lies. He shoots piercing daggers at it like the look he had toward me when I first saw him. His eyes shift from Charles's hand to my crossed legs—not just where my legs are crossed but higher. He is looking at my sex. I clench underneath my clothes and fight the urge to shift while he's staring at me.

I clear my throat, trying to ease the dryness I feel, before I answer their next question. They repeat the question for Guy to answer, but he doesn't move. He stays fixated on my thighs.

"Mr. Harrington," the male investigator asks a little louder.

Guy snaps out of it and removes his eyes from my body. He inhales sharply before saying, "I'm sorry. I'm still a little tired from the whole thing. Can you repeat the question?"

The interview lasts almost two hours. I am eager to get everyone out the door, so I purposely make polite, curt good-byes and don't ask any questions or make any statements that might prompt them to want to talk more.

The investigators thank us for our time. They believe the crash was caused by a defective fan blade from one of the allied signal engines that was severed from the left turbine where it caused a complete engine failure—a lot of words I hardly know the meaning of. But they remind us the investigation can't be closed unless we have a full health evaluation. They ask if I can make sure that gets done as soon as possible.

"Tomorrow morning is my appointment," I assure them.

Satisfied, they walk out the front door with Guy in tow.

"Mr. Harrington, can you wait a moment?" Charles chimes in and keeps him from leaving our home.

# Twenty-Five

"Please, call me Guy, Mr. Devereux."

Charles smiles. "All right, Guy. Then, please call me Charles."

They each extend their hands and shake as they nod. Sealing the deal on how to address each other.

I feel flush and faint. "Charles, please don't keep him. I'm sure his wife is waiting for him to get back to her." I can't help but look at Guy when I say, "She was really happy to see him return home safely yesterday."

"No, I won't keep you," Charles answers my request while looking at Guy. "I just wanted to thank you for all you did for my wife."

Guy's eyes move softly over to me. "It was my pleasure."

*Oh, I feel sick.*

The way he said *pleasure* penetrated me in a way it shouldn't have. The muscles between my legs clench again, and an uncomfortable pit in my stomach forms.

My heart begins to race, and heat rises in my body. The room begins to spin. Everything becomes blurry before I can't see anything at all. I know I'm falling to the ground, but I can't feel or see.

The light in the room is blurred as I try to open my eyes. My head is pounding, and I feel like I'm out of body.

I blink, trying to force my eyes to focus. There's a figure in front of me.

"Charles," I moan. But, as soon as I say it, I realize my mistake.

"No, it's me," Guy whispers and runs his hand over the top of my head. "You sure have a knack for fainting in front of me. I think this is the third time." He's speaking low, and I don't see Charles in the room.

I've been moved to the living room, and I can feel the leather under my back from our tufted sofa.

"Are you okay?" Guy whispers again.

My hand moves down to my stomach, and I try to think about how my body is feeling, how my baby is feeling, after a fall like that.

"You hit your head," he explains.

"I don't care." I shake my head, and Guy seems confused. "I'm just worried about …"

Guy's eyes move, and he fights the urge to put his hands on my middle. I'm not sure if either one of us could handle his hands touching me so close to my core.

"It must be why I fainted."

"Why haven't you seen a doctor?" He looks concerned.

"Because I don't want to be wrong about being pregnant," I regretfully say. "But I'll go tomorrow."

I try to sit up, looking for Charles, but Guy stops me by reaching across and holding my shoulders down.

"No," he says, still whispering. "You need to rest."

"Why are you whispering, and where is my husband?" I ask him, trying to look around while I'm forced to lie on the couch. I don't trust myself being in a room alone with Guy.

"You haven't told him, have you?" he asks, averting his eyes to my stomach.

"No, there hasn't been a good time," I answer, feeling more awake and increasingly irritated. "And you didn't answer my question. Where is my *husband*?" The emphasis of my desperate plea for my *husband* seems to bring pain to Guy's face.

He pulls his body up and further away from me. His lips twitch with anger, but he controls his temper. "I've been whispering because I saw an opportunity where I was alone with you, and I took it. *I* don't hate you now that we're in New York."

My hand grabs his wrist. "I don't hate you," I strongly whisper, trying to defend myself. "I just need to—"

"She's awake," Guy yells and yanks his hand free of mine.

"I don't mean to hurt you. I just—" I try to quickly whisper to him, but Charles dashes into the room, replacing Guy's body in front of me with his.

Just like that, Guy is out of the way, and my husband is back by my side.

"Where were you?" I asked.

"On the phone with the doctor, but he said, as long as you woke up and felt fine, we wouldn't need to go to the emergency room," Charles explains to me.

I move my eyes to where Guy is now standing just to the left, behind Charles.

He sends a warning with his eyes, telling me to go see the doctor as soon as possible. But I'm so uncomfortable and feeling confused with these two men in the room; I just want this moment to go away and move on. I'll see the doctor as planned, tomorrow.

"I'm fine," I reassure Charles and then move my eyes up to Guy. "I'm fine," I repeat for his benefit.

Guy closes his eyes, and a flood of relief seems to run through him. Charles is relieved as well. I try to sit up, but I go slowly so as not to cause any more worry from either of the men.

"Are you sure you're feeling well enough to sit, darling? You can keep resting," Charles says with his hand on my back.

"No, no, I'm fine. I'm really fine." I can feel the blood running through my body normally now, and everything seems to be as it was before I fainted. "I just got light-headed; that's all."

"Of course, honey," Charles says and rubs his hand in a circle.

I swallow the saliva that's gathered in my mouth. I feel nervous to say it, but it has to be said. "We need to let Guy get back to his wife. I'm sure he doesn't need to be kept here any longer than we've already detained him."

"Of course," Charles says and then looks over to Guy. "I've got it from here, but I appreciate all the help you've given my wife."

His jaw seems tight and tense, but he manages to speak as if there were no discomfort, "It was no problem." He looks pointedly at me. "Now that I know you're okay, I should get going."

I nod, agreeing. My body loves when he's near, but my nerves can't handle it. I can't have him in my home and talking with my husband any longer.

With Charles's help, I stand up from the couch and walk with the men to the foyer. I need to give Guy a final good-bye.

Feeling shy, I look down when Guy and Charles speak to each other.

The men shake hands once more, and Guy turns to look at me.

"Naomi"—he dips his head to bring my attention fully up to his face—"I wish nothing but the best for you and your family." His eyes quickly dart down to my center and then back up to my eyes.

I inhale slowly and let it out just as slow. "Thank you," I reply.

My appreciation is for what I think he's trying to tell me—that he understands Charles and I are likely going to have a baby and that he won't get in the way of our family. At least, I hope that's what he's trying to say.

I step in to hug him and wrap my arms around his still-hard body, loosely but with warmth and meaning. I inhale his scent. There's cleanliness and expensive cologne, but his true scent is still there, underneath it all. It's intoxicating. I close my eyes to savor it. This might be the last time I experience his scent and feel his body near me. It makes me sad.

This isn't any typical hug good-bye; this is a *good-bye* hug—for likely forever.

"Thank you," I repeat before letting him go and watching him walk out the door.

# Twenty-Six

Something feels as if it's slipped away once the door closes behind him. A loss maybe. I wish I could just forget what happened between us and what I grew to feel for Guy, but first, I have to face it before I can forget it. If I don't tell my husband, it will eat away at me until I go crazy.

"We'll have to get together with him and his wife for dinner," Charles suggests as we walk out of the foyer.

I sigh. "I imagine his wife has a busy schedule." I look up at Charles. "She's a model, you know. And their marriage isn't exactly stable."

"Oh, that's too bad," he says without any hint of care or emotion.

I feel as if I'm chock-full of emotion. Jealousy, for one, at the thought of Guy's perfect model wife. And sadness because I want Guy to be happy. I can't help but compare myself to his seemingly perfect wife. What would he want with me anyway?

He said he loved me, but I was his only option when we were alone together on the island.

*Oh God.* The thought of Guy and the memory of our bodies intertwined come back to me. I remember him thrusting himself inside me and making me scream when I came.

*How could I have these thoughts in the presence of my husband?* I want to crawl under a rock, ashamed of myself and my body's reaction.

The guilt is weighing too heavily on me.

I reach down and hold my husband's hand. "Will you come with me to my doctor's appointment tomorrow morning?"

He looks at me as if I didn't have to ask. "Of course," he says, not realizing the real importance of the appointment.

*What have I done to deserve such a wonderful man?*

I don't deserve him. Not after what I did with Guy.

"There's something I want to talk to you about," I quietly tell him, trying to be strong.

His eyes light up. "Oh, yes, there was something I wanted to show you before everyone arrived." He pulls my hand and leads me down the long hallway. "Come here, and I'll show you. It'll have to be quick because Mother is expecting us at the house."

I scoff. "What? Why?"

"She's happy about your homecoming, too, darling. She has been worried about you, and she's planning a welcome-home lunch. Your parents and Samantha will also be there."

We reach the entrance to the study, but I stop him before going in.

"But, honey, I really feel like we need to stay home and talk. There are some important things I need to tell you."

He holds my arms, just below my shoulders. "I'm sorry, darling. I should have asked you first, but it's not something I can reschedule now." He runs the pad of his thumb on my forehead. "It will be just the two of us tonight, okay?" He leans down and kisses my head.

*Charles is my best friend. There is nothing I can't tell him. He will understand. It will be fine*, I keep telling myself on repeat, hoping my words are true.

"Okay," I agree. "Now, what did you need to show me?"

There are a few documents sitting on the center of his desk. Charles picks them up and hands them to me. My eyes scan the pages. I look up at him with bewilderment.

"You paid for all the school supplies for the entire county?"

He softly smiles and nods.

My first thought is, *I have to get back to work.*

"So, they didn't work out a budget for the school supplies."

"It's all taken care of," he reassures me.

"For now," I say almost to myself.

Charles looks confused. "Darling, I thought you'd be happy. I thought this would help."

I sigh, realizing how ungrateful I must seem. "I am happy. Thank you, Charles. But I need to get back to work as soon as possible because, if the school district didn't work out a budget for the supplies, then they will have the same problem next year. We're just delaying the inevitable if we can't come up with a solid funding process or get the school district to rearrange the priorities in their budget."

Charles draws out an exhausted breath. "I was trying to help."

*By cutting a check.* Being a Devereux, he has no idea people have to work for something. I saw the injustice and I've been working hard to change the system for years, and I just spent six weeks working hard to survive.

But none of that is his fault.

"I'm sorry, honey." I place my hand on his arm. "This is thoughtful, and I don't deserve such a generous husband."

He puts his arm around me and draws me into him.

"It's all right." He forgives me. "It's not like you to be so agitated. I'd insist you take another bath to relax and de-stress from what you went through if we didn't have to be at Mother's soon."

My tears fall out and absorb into his shirt. I'm so grateful for his efforts, but for some reason, I feel miles apart from him.

We dress the same for lunch at the manor as we do dinner at Le Cirque. Casual wear must be banned because even Gwendelyn's staff has formal attire during the day. My parents know the drill, and I imagine they will be spruced up as well.

I never got my driver's license when I was a teenager. There was no need for cars when I was in undergraduate school and again working for my master's. We've lived in New York City our entire adult lives.

When we step out of the building, I feel struck by all the loud sounds. Horns blaring, people shouting, construction drills, even the sound of my own high heels on the concrete sound like screeches in my head. I wince and cover my ears with my hands.

"What's wrong, love?" Charles asks.

I shake my head and try to breathe through the irritation. "It's fine." I take my hands down. "I'm just not used to all the noise." Now that the adrenaline from being rescued is gone, I realize how foreign civilization is to me. I never would have thought it was something I'd have to get used to again.

Our town car pulls up to the curb just outside our building lobby. The doorman opens the car door for me, and Charles travels around to the other side to get in. There are water bottles placed in the leather armrest between us. Magazines are in the back of the seat in front of me. A *New York Times* waits for Charles in front of him.

As the car begins to move forward, I pick up the magazines and place them on my lap. Starting with the one on top, I flip through the cover and start to read each page, hoping to pass the time for our forty-five-minute commute.

Nothing has changed since I've been gone. The celebrities are all the same. The movies and music and books are all the same ones people were raving about in the magazines I read on the way to Turks and Caicos. In fact, I've only missed one month of subscriptions.

*How can I feel like I was gone for so long, but so little time has passed here?*

Only eight pages into *People* magazine, I see *him*. Actually, I see her first, but he's right there behind her.

The color blue is featured on the celebrity style page. Jessica Chastain, Kate Winslet, Miranda Kerr, Michelle Williams, Helen Mirren, and Marina Cary are all wearing gorgeous blue gowns. Marina's is a dazzling, sequined mermaid figure that hugs the tight curves of her lower body after leaving the plunging neckline that almost reaches her belly. She wears it so well and with so much confidence. I could never pull anything like that off, and even if my body could hold it up, I couldn't. I would feel far too self-conscious and out of place to wear anything like that to any event.

Behind her are several people, but he is unmistakable to me now. He stands with his hands in his tuxedo pants pockets. Instead of looking at his pristine wife, he's looking at someone else. I shake my head at him on the page, and I continue to shake it back and forth at myself for being equally as foolish of a person.

*I'm just another woman he cheated on his wife with.* The thought makes me feel cheap.

I hastily shove the magazine back in the pocket in front of me. Charles glances at me but doesn't say anything.

I grab another magazine, *Departures*—sent to us for our American Express account. A few articles in, there's a spread on Machu Picchu in Peru. The Andes Mountains is lush with bright green grass in front of sprawling stone walls.

"It's beautiful," I whisper to myself.

Charles eyes me, still holding his paper in front. "Everything okay, darling?" he asks.

"Yes," I reassure him. "What do you think about going hiking? Maybe in a few days, we could get out of the city, go up north, and get some fresh air? Maybe see a beautiful view?"

"Hiking?" he asks, surprised and trying to suppress a chuckle. "I think you've had enough adventure, don't you?"

Forcing a smile, I nod lightly. The thing is, I'm not sure I have.

Putting the magazine back, I pick up the *New York Post* instead. And there they are again. The entertainment section is hosting an article on how Marina is searching for her missing husband. I scoff to myself as I read the part about how they have such a loving marriage. Far from the truth, I know. But then I become sorrowful when I see a picture of them from before the plane crash. They both look gorgeous, and Marina certainly seems happy. Guy seems happy, too—to the untrained eye. But I know better. There is an intensity in his eyes that I have gotten to know so well. It's missing in this picture.

I slam the pages closed on my lap.

"Sorry, honey," I say to Charles after realizing I startled him. "I'm just not in the mood to read right now."

He pats my knee before going back into his paper. "Okay, honey. We're almost there anyway."

I am surprised that Gwendelyn is actually somewhat happy to see me safe and sound.

Once we arrive, she pulls me aside and says, "Charles has never been more devastated. So, for that, I'm very grateful that you're home."

I take her compliment. No point in opening up old wounds when she's trying to be more pleasant toward me. If it's not blatantly rude, I'll take it.

My mother and father are here as well as Samantha.

As soon as I walked in the door, they showered me with the love and attention they thought I needed.

What I really need is to be left alone with my husband. I need time to think and then to explain everything. I need time to tell him how wonderful and enriched our lives will be with a baby along the way, and I need time to break his heart and tell him about my affair with Guy on the island.

The door to the sunroom opens and catches my eye. It's one of the staff members. He leans into Gwendelyn's ear and says something as he hands her a newspaper clipping. She nods a thank-you, and he walks out the way he came.

Samantha hands out a champagne glass filled with orange juice, and of course, the bubbles tell me champagne is in there, too.

"No, thank you," I tell her. "I'm not in the mood to drink."

"You're not pregnant, are you?" she exclaims a little too loudly.

Everyone in the room looks at me. Even the staff stops moving and stares, waiting for an answer. Charles's head tilts, curious about Samantha's outburst. I wonder if he's thinking about the possibility. I want to tell him and shout across the room, but I can't. If I begin to speak, I know I'll stutter. If he were the only one here, I'd tell him everything I need to confess. But this is not the time or place in front of all these people.

Gwendelyn has an equally inquisitive expression on her face. Everyone is looking at me, anticipating my answer, but she's demanding one from me.

"N-no, of course not," I finally announce to the room.

# *Twenty-Seven*

Charles lets out a breath but then smiles softly at me, telling me that it'll be okay. *We'll get pregnant eventually, darling*, he says with his eyes.

Gwendelyn appears relieved for a moment but then purses her lips in my direction. Her reaction surprises me since I've been under the impression she has been pining for a grandchild for years now. An heir to satisfy her family's longevity.

"Oh God, I'm so sorry," Samantha lowers her voice to say. "That was awkward and not my business."

I try to smile to put her mind at ease, but my lips tremble. Seeing my reaction, Samantha lightly grips my arm and turns me away from the room.

We're standing in the corner of the sunroom, which has all the light and decor of a garden but is sealed off to preserve the air-conditioning.

"I'm sorry," she repeats. "Are you okay?"

I shake my head, fighting the tears.

She hones in on me and sternly looks at me. "You know you can tell me anything."

Again, I shake my head. "I know," I let out. "It's just something I really need to speak to Charles about before telling anyone else."

Being with such a good friend, knowing I can confide in her, makes it hard to hold back my secrets. I want to tell her, but it wouldn't be right.

"I was a different person on that island," I confess to her. "But I can't talk about it with you yet."

She opens her arms and hugs me. "I understand. I'm here for you whenever you need me. Okay?"

Samantha knows just about everything about me. She understands, even when I need to keep something from her. Other than Charles, she's my best friend … and a good one.

"I wonder if I could have a word with you." Gwendelyn's voice crackles behind me, like nails on a chalkboard.

Still embracing Samantha, I bring my hand up to my eye and wipe the impending tear trying to escape. The last thing I want is for Gwendelyn to know that I'm emotional.

"Of course," I tell her, letting go of my friend and turning to face my mother-in-law.

Gwendelyn gives me a curt smile and then turns after saying, "Let's find someplace more private."

I dutifully follow my mother-in-law but not after giving Samantha a pleading look for help. I know she can't do anything about Gwendelyn. It would be foolish for her to stand up to her or anyone else for that matter. But Samantha knows what to do. She'll casually mention to Charles that his mother has swept me away somewhere for a discussion. Charles will come to my rescue, like he always does when his mother is concerned.

She leads me into the formal sitting room where the coffered wood beams match the tiny detailed etching surrounding the large fireplace. The room is rich with money, but the floral and gold-trimmed furniture dates the decor. But, since it still screams wealth, Gwendelyn won't be changing it anytime soon.

"Something has been brought to my attention," she slowly lets out while taking a seat on the sofa, prompting me to sit opposite her.

"Oh?" I try to feign casualness. The trick with her is to not let her think she's getting to you.

"I don't think it's a secret that I've never cared for you being married to my son."

My head picks up, and I sit more erect, showing her my confidence and strength against her brutal accusations that are sure to come.

"I'm sure you're aware," she goes on to say, "that you won't get a dime of Charles's family money if infidelity is ever an issue. Just because you didn't sign a prenuptial agreement doesn't mean my legal team can't protect my son and his family name."

My heart beats faster, and nerves circulate throughout my body like an out-of-control beehive. But I breathe deep and try to appear strong and confident.

*She doesn't know what she's talking about,* I try to convince myself. Now, I also need to convince her of that.

"I love Charles," I say, beginning to defend myself. "I would never." I stand up on my shaking legs to let her know I'm finished with this conversation and that I'm not waiting around for more.

"Sit down," she commands. Her fragile old voice becomes frightening at a higher volume.

Even I, a grown woman, am afraid of her wrath.

I do as she said, worried the situation will get worse if I defy her any more than I already have.

Her eyes peer down to the table in between us. She picks up a black-and-white newspaper; it's this morning's *New York Times*. She hands me a section.

"Like I said, something has been brought to my attention," she says, watching me look at the article.

It's about my rescue. The article is a quarter of a page long, but then it mentions that the story continues on another page. I flip the paper over, looking for more of the article, but this is all she's given me.

"I'm not sure what you're trying to prove. We all know that I was in a plane crash and lost for a month and a half." I slap the paper back down; I'm at a loss for what she feels she has over me.

Immediately, she bends forward to pick the paper back up. "I'm not concerned with the words, dear. It's this picture that has piqued my interest."

Her pointed, manicured finger taps over the two photos shown. One is of the plane that brought us home. The hatch is open, and I'm standing just behind the left of the pilot. Guy has his arm wrapped around me. We're waiting for the stairs to connect to the aircraft. That was when Guy held me back. In this photo, you can see he's holding my stomach and whispering in my ear. If you look close enough—and I have no doubts that Gwendelyn has—you can see the intimacy of the gesture.

My voice cracks when I say, "I was trying to get to my husband."

Her accusations might be too close for comfort, but there is no proof.

"That man you see there is keeping me from jumping out of the plane."

"Mmhmm," she curtly hums. "Yes, the way he is touching you and seemingly speaking into your ear does appear to be on a more intimate level. But what really gives it away is this picture." Her fingernail taps over the second photo.

I look down, swallowing what confidence I might have had. The photo is of me crying and embracing Charles. It must have been taken shortly after our reunion. Only Gwendelyn could turn something that's supposed to be a beautiful moment into an ugly accusation.

But then I see past us, and my breath leaves my body. I've been so worried about how I'm going to be breaking my husband's heart that I've been completely naive to the heart I've already broken.

*I thought I was just another lay.*

"It's more than that," Guy told me so many times on the island. He even went as far as to tell me he loves me.

But I didn't listen. At least, I didn't take him seriously.

Guy was passing by when the photo was taken. The look on his face can't be mistaken. The pain he feels as he looks down on me reuniting with my husband is palpable and hard for me to deny.

"This proves nothing, Gwendelyn." I raise my voice an octave higher and stand up again.

This time, she stands up, too.

"You slept with that man, didn't you?" she demands.

I want to scream, *No, no, no*, but I'd be betraying the truth, and in this very moment, I'm not thinking clearly enough to lie.

"That is—" I'm about to tell her it's none of her business, which couldn't be truer, but I can feel my confidence draining.

"I noticed you didn't have any champagne," she goes on to say. "Are you pregnant? Because, if so, that child will have nothing to do with my son or this family. You've disgraced us, and you're nothing more than a common whore."

My whole body shakes. "You've got it all wrong!" I shout.

But then I'm soon startled by an even louder rant.

"Complete and utter bullshit!" Charles yells. His face is red, the vein on his forehead is bulging, and his anger is directed straight at his mother. His eyes are honed in on her, and he's visibly upset.

He descends the two steps into the sunken room. "Mother, that is enough!" His voice makes the room vibrate with his intensity. "You've gone too far this time."

Her hand delicately flies up to her chest, and she lowers her voice to a soft, motherly tone. "Charles, I'm just looking out for you. She has clearly betrayed you."

"That's enough," he repeats. "Naomi would never betray me."

Hearing him say that makes my heart ache. I don't even deserve a heart anymore.

This is what I wanted. I wanted him to come to my rescue and save me from his mother, but her accusations couldn't possibly hurt as badly as Charles falsely defending me.

"I trust her," he goes on to say. "And, if you can't do that, then I have no room for you in my life."

Gwendelyn is stunned and speechless. Charles has stood up to her in the past, but he has never offered an ultimatum like this.

I can't let him do this. I can't let him make a fool of himself on my behalf any longer.

I grab his hand. "Honey, let's just go. We need to leave."

As I'm crying and pleading with him to let go of this argument with his mother, he sees the desperation on my face.

Nodding, he agrees.

"I just want to go home right now," I beg him. *And tell you everything*, I add in my mind.

Hand in hand, with our backs turned, we walk away from Gwendelyn. An unrecognizable shaking voice calls out to Charles, but we both ignore it as we continue out of the home.

We don't say good-bye to my parents, Samantha, or Charles's other family who was able to come. We just leave.

I can text my mom and Sam tomorrow. I'll definitely need their support then more than ever.

# Twenty-Eight

I can't bring myself to utter a word in the car. I'm feeling too ashamed, and Charles seems too angry to speak. Plus, I can't bear starting something here and then needing to move up to our apartment.

My confession is something that needs to be done delicately, especially now that he's defended me against his mother.

Our town car pulls up in front of our building, but there are too many people and flashes of light for me to see the doorman.

"What the hell is going on here?" Charles says, as agitated as I've ever seen him.

I'm sure he's still on edge after confronting his mother, and now, this …

I can only make out the doorman's arm near our car before the door becomes slightly ajar.

He's yelling at them, "Get back. Give the lady some space!" He forces it open enough for me to squeeze out.

Charles got out on the other side and came around to help the doorman assist me.

"Mrs. Devereux, what was it like, being on a deserted island for forty-two days?" one reporter yells as I try to walk through the crowd.

I'm not safe until I get into the security of my own building. I turn to look outside and realize that the crowd is actually very small. They just hovered around me and invaded my personal space to the point where I had no room to breathe.

Upstairs in our apartment, Charles is fuming into his phone. "I told them, no stories. I asked for our privacy. This is a very private family, and we do not appreciate the press lurking at our door. Hasn't my wife been through enough?" He paces back and forth in the living room. "Henry, I am holding you personally accountable."

Henry is our publicist, the one the Devereuxes hire to keep their name out of the papers. I imagine how Gwendelyn will blame this all on me, adding another log to the blazing fire.

"He did what?" Charles shouts into the phone.

I can't help but stand up at full attention.

He tugs at his cashmere vest, too hot for the material. He frustratingly puts his phone down. He pulls his vest over his head and tosses it on one of the living room chairs. "Damn," he spits with his hands on his hips.

"Charles, what is it?" I move to be near him.

"It's Guy Harrington."

I stop in my tracks. My stomach feels like it's jumped into my heart. "Why? Wh-what's wrong? What have you heard?"

He shakes his head, disappointed. "It's him or his wife. Someone from their camp sent the photogs and reporters to our door. They gave them information about you, wanting to share your story."

"But we've said, no interviews," I whine.

"I know, darling. But, for some reason, they told the press that you wanted to share your experience on the island."

"I don't." I begin to wildly shake my head. "I don't. I really don't."

Charles moves closer and places his arms around me. "I know, darling. It will be fine. Henry will fix it for us." He rests his chin on the top of my head. "I think I'll give Guy Harrington a call, so we can set this straight. Maybe invite him back over, so we can discuss it."

"No!" My head pops back up, and I look up to Charles.

He seems confused by my reaction and peculiarly looks down on me.

"I just think it's best to let the professionals handle it," I explain.

Charles releases me and moves toward his phone. "Nonsense. No point in using middlemen when we can solve this issue like men." He picks it up and holds it in his palm as if he's going to scroll for a number. "I have his contact information from the investigators."

"Honey," I say cautiously, as if he were holding a bomb. "Honey, put the phone down. I need to talk to you about something."

He puts his finger on his cell phone while it's ringing, waiting for Guy to answer. "Just one moment, honey. This won't take long."

"Hello?" On the other end, I hear that familiar, deep voice that whispered dirty things in my ear on the island.

"Put the goddamn phone down!" I yell with my fists trembling by my sides.

# Twenty-Nine

Suddenly, I feel like all the blood in my body is at a standstill. Charles grasps the seriousness of the situation and slowly does as I said, placing his phone back down on the side table, hanging up on Guy.

"Naomi, what's going on? What have you not told me?"

I wonder if he knows what I'm about to tell him, if he believes anything his mother said at all or if this will be a complete and utter surprise.

My hand continues to tremble as the words unsteadily come out of my mouth, "I'm so sorry."

Charles emotionally readies himself for a blow. His stance changes, his posture, everything morphs into someone who can see they are about to hear something they never wanted to hear. "What exactly are you sorry about?"

I want to be closer to him, but my body can't move. "I didn't mean for it to happen. I didn't know we were ever going to be rescued." My mouth quivers as I speak.

Charles just stands there and sharpens his focus on me, expecting me to continue. "Naomi, what did you do?"

"Charles, honey, let's sit down, and I can explain everything." I step back toward the couch and hope that he moves forward to sit with me.

His legs shift, but he doesn't make any progress in my direction. "I think I'd rather stand, and I think I'd rather hear what you have to say sooner than later. Naomi, please tell me what the hell happened. You're scaring me."

I'm not sure my body will hold. I bend my knees and allow myself to sit on the sofa underneath me. I can't believe I'm going to say it. I can't believe the words are going to come out of my mouth.

I bury my face in my hands and mumble, "I slept with him."

"What did you say?" Charles asks calmly but shaking with devastation.

I open my mouth to suck in air, but it only comes in choppy, sputtering chunks. "I'm so sorry," I manage.

"What did you say?" he repeats more forcefully.

With my jaw trembling, "I slept with him," squeaks out with more volume, and I instantly see the confirmed devastation on my husband's face.

He takes a step back and places his hand on the chair back. His chest, weighted, moves up and down in a labored but exerted fashion.

I stand up. "I'm so sorry, Charles. Will you let me explain?" My chest heaves, matching his. "I didn't think I was ever going to leave. I didn't think I was ever going to see you again. I didn't want to, but then …"

"It was a month, Naomi. Don't make excuses as if you were gone for seven years." He turns and paces in a circle. "A month!" he yells again.

"Six weeks," I correct him.

Leaning forward, I reach my hands out to him, asking for mercy. "It felt like forever." I beg him for understanding.

"But it wasn't." He swipes his hands down, swatting my hands away. "It wasn't forever. Not even close. It was forty-two days, and you slept with someone."

"You don't know what it was like on that island. Time felt different there. *I* felt different there."

Charles darts his finger in my direction. "*You* don't know what it was like here, finding ways to search for you day in and day out." He spins around, unable to face me. "You have no idea what *I've* been through."

"You threw money at it, Charles. You wrote a check and waited for the Coast Guard, other people, to do the work. I had to *survive*."

I feel the tears start to burn my skin. He has no idea what I went through. I can't blame him. Guy is the only one who could possibly understand what it was like, being stranded.

But I can't defend myself. I know I did such a horrible and maybe unforgivable thing.

Charles stands in the middle of the room and holds his hand over his chest, scrunching his knuckles as if he were trying to grip something in there.

*I've broken his heart.*

He can feel it, and I can see it. A part of my own heart breaks along with him.

He eventually moves to take a seat in one of the chairs opposite the sofa. We're not used to arguing, so we sit there in silence for over an hour. Charles massages his chest every now and then, and I sob quietly on and off.

I'm afraid to speak to him, afraid to make it worse. I want to tell him about the baby, but I imagined, when I did tell him, it would be a happy time. I don't believe anything can make this a happy time.

Charles shakes his head with his hands sprawled across the smooth crest of where his hair should be. He looks up to me for the first time in over an hour. He finds my eyes and stands up. "I don't think I should be here right now. I need a little time to think. I'm going to stay at my mother's."

*Oh no. Anything but Gwendelyn.*

The last thing I need is for her to think she was right. She wasn't right. She has no idea what went on between Guy and me on that island, and neither does Charles. I can't allow my husband to be around Gwendelyn's influence at a moment like this. It will ruin us for sure and solidify the damage I've done to our marriage. I can't let that happen.

I know what I have to do to keep him from leaving right now.

"Charles, you can't," I muster out while trying to sniffle away the pressure that's built up in my nose.

He turns to walk away. With his back to me, he says determinedly, "I can, and I will."

I quickly stand and desperately reach in his direction. "I'm pregnant," I call out to him.

He immediately stops in his tracks.

His shoulders hunch to a new low. He slowly turns around to face me head-on once again. Before, I could see the solid pain inside him. Now, his pain is met with tears flowing softly down his face.

He places his hand over his chest again. "Are you trying to kill me?" he asks.

I want to go to him. I want to be in his arms for this moment so badly. I've dreamed of it for so long. But I know he won't allow me there.

"No, no. Of course not," I try to plea with him.

But, before I have a chance to explain, Charles raises his voice. "Is it even mine?" he yells.

As I'm flustered, my hands begin to shake again. "I-I-I—yes. Of course! Yes, it's yours, Charles. Your mother is wrong; she's so wrong about me."

"How?" he quickly snaps. As he's fighting with something inside himself, his hand goes up to his head, and his fingers spread across his face. "You've been with another man, and now, you're pregnant?"

"Charles, look at me," I beg.

Reluctantly, he removes his hand from his face.

"Remember the night before I left? I think, this time, it worked. I think we're going to have a baby."

He shakes his head, pacing across the floor. "Don't do this to me, Naomi. All I can hear you say is, *think*. What am I supposed to *think* when you tell me you slept with someone else, and you're pregnant with our child?" He spins around in frustration. "Well, are you, or aren't you?"

I look down and allow my tears to fall to the floor. "I have an appointment tomorrow."

When I take a step toward him, he doesn't move, but his stare tells me that I've reached my boundary, and I don't dare get any closer.

"Don't leave me, Charles. Come with me to the appointment tomorrow."

He places his hands on his hips and looks up to the wood-paneled ceiling. "I never thought I would want to leave you. Of all the people in the world, I never thought you would do something so stupid. I never thought you would hurt me like this." He brings his head down to look at me. "I never thought you would hurt *us*."

That is his closing remark. Charles turns around and walks out the door with me pleading him not to go.

I spend the rest of the day sulking, closed off from the world in Charles's and my bedroom.

Kathy was at the store while we argued, but she knows not to disturb me with our door locked.

All I can do now is hope and pray that Charles shows up to the doctor's appointment in the morning. I need him now more than ever.

I sent Charles three text messages and called twice, only leaving one voice message. I haven't heard a word.

He knows where to find me.

But, now, he'll have to find me at the doctor's appointment in Midtown. I'll have to go alone.

Leaving my apartment, I scan the streets before having our doorman call me a car, hoping Charles is near, just needing more fresh air before seeing me again. But I only see a woman walking her dog and a man leaning against the building across the street. No Charles.

The room smells as sterile and dry as my heart feels right now. I should be happy, anticipating this moment. Charles should be happy, but he's not even here with me.

I sit legs crossed with my purse in my lap, just staring straight ahead, waiting for my name to be called. He didn't come home last night. I can only imagine he went to his mother's. What he told her, I have no idea. I'm sure she's satisfied, knowing she was right—at least, partly. The separation and the unknown are killing me.

"Mrs. Devereux," a young woman in pink teddy bear–patterned scrubs calls my name.

When I begin to move, she looks at me and smiles. I try to smile back, but I wonder if my pain shows through instead. I've never been very good at hiding my emotions.

She leads me out of the waiting room and down a carpeted hall. The patient rooms are on the left, but she gestures her hand to the right, pointing toward the lonely door after the nurses' station.

"We'll need a urine sample." She looks at the papers attached to the clipboard in her hand. "And I see we're doing a pregnancy test as well as a full blood workup and physical." She questioningly looks at me.

I nod. "Yes, that is correct."

"Okay then." She smiles. "Your pregnancy results will be available within a few minutes. You'll be in room B." She hands me a plastic cup. "When you're done, place the cup in the door above the toilet and then wait for the doctor in your room. He should be in shortly after you're finished."

I take the cup from her hand and begin following through with her instructions.

After peeing into the cup, I turn around and open the little silver door with a black latch. I place the cup on the little wooden shelf.

*This is so impersonal, so disenchanting, and unromantic.*

Putting my gown on in a lonely room, I wonder what I really want. My light-blue one-size-fits-all gown remains untied in the back since there is no one here to help me secure it closed.

It shouldn't be like this. This is supposed to be a happy time where Charles and I are here together because we love each other, and we want to welcome a baby into our lives. I never planned to be a single mom. I've never even thought about it until now. What I wanted was to have a child with my husband.

On the other hand, if Charles finds it in his heart to forgive me, I'll always question if we are together for the baby and not because he wants to be with me.

I'm damned either way, and I hate feeling this way about being pregnant.

I take in a deep breath and compose myself when I hear a knock at the door.

"Come in," I call.

My breath stills in my lungs, as I'm hoping and anticipating that I see my husband's face come through that door.

Disappointed when I see a white coat, I slowly exhale the breath I was holding through my nose.

"Mrs. Devereux, I'm Dr. Braxton," he introduces himself.

As the door closes behind him, he reaches out his hand. I move to shake his, but our greeting is interrupted when the door stops before it shuts.

Those long fingers curve around the door, and Charles's gentle eyes peer through the small space left.

"Hello," he cautiously says while opening the door a little more.

"Hi." I try to match his gentleness, coaxing him to come all the way into the room and be near me.

He steps in, still cautious and wearing the pain I saw him in yesterday.

The doctor spins in Charles's direction. "Hello. You must be Mr. Devereux."

"I am," Charles confirms.

Dr. Braxton gives Charles a puzzling smile. I imagine he is picking up on the tension in the room.

"I bet you're happy to have your wife back."

Not looking away from the doctor, Charles licks his lips, hesitating. I know he's searching himself for an honest answer.

"Of course I am," he finally says.

A wave of relief washes through me, but I know this storm isn't over. It's only the beginning of a long road toward reconciliation. But at least he has given me a sign that, even though I hurt him, I still mean more to him than just someone who betrayed him.

"Well, please take a seat. I was just about to go over some things with your wife."

Charles takes a seat in one of two chairs against the wall. I wish he were closer, but I'll take what I can get. I watch him as he moves. He doesn't look at me. I can't even see him fighting the urge to look my way.

Dr. Braxton clears his throat, demanding my attention again. "I'm glad your husband is able to join us." He leans back against the countertop opposite the hospital bed I'm sitting on. Crossing his arms, he continues, "Your pregnancy result has come back negative."

It takes me a second to process what he said.

*Negative.*

"I'm not pregnant?"

He shakes his head. "No, dear. I'm sorry, you're not."

"But I haven't had my period. It's been over two months since my last period. We've been trying to get pregnant for six months."

I knew I didn't know for sure. I knew I needed confirmation, but it felt impossible for me to be wrong. All the facts added up. I should be pregnant.

The doctor gives me one slow nod. "Well, that's part of why we need this full examination after what you've been through. It was a big ordeal, and your body … and mind," he adds, "have been through a traumatic experience. It's not uncommon for a woman to skip a whole month, even several months, during such stressful times."

"B-but, but …" I desperately look for something else to prove him wrong. He has to be wrong about this. "I threw up the other night. I was nauseous from the pizza."

I look at Charles, so he can help me confirm my case, but he's just staring off. No reaction.

"For forty-two days, you lived off of little food and no variety to your food choices. You survived, but you were malnourished. It's a natural reaction for your body to reject some foods that used to bring you comfort. You were in fight-or-flight mode on that island, and you adjusted to survive. Now that you are back home, you are feeling the effects of what you went through."

*He has no idea what I went through and the effects it's having on me. I feel like I'm losing my mind.*

"But … I fainted yesterday," I continue to argue, grasping on to the hope I had of being pregnant.

Charles stands up. "You are not pregnant, Naomi," he angrily spits his words out.

Wide-eyed, I look at him and watch him turn around and leave the room.

The sterile scent of the clean white room feels dirty to me now. I feel dirty, and everything I touch turns to ugliness. My face falls into my hands, and I begin to weep in front of the doctor.

He moves to the side of the bed I'm sitting on and places his hand on my back. "Mrs. Devereux, I can't begin to understand what you've been through. Your wounds go more than skin deep. That is why your physical examination is only part of your analysis and healing process. I think it would be beneficial if your husband joined you for some counseling sessions."

"I don't need counseling," I mumble into my hands between sobs. "My husband probably doesn't want anything to do with me anymore."

His hand moves in a circular motion on my back. "I'm sure that's not true."

I don't bother arguing with him. The last thing I want is to explain the horrible thing that I did.

"This has been a traumatic experience for him in a different way. Nonetheless, your healing process might take a lot longer than the six weeks you had to endure out there. You might be dealing with emotional issues indefinitely. That's something you need to address and begin sessions for immediately."

"How?" I pick my head up from my hands. "How? How can something that felt like forever but only lasted forty-two days affect me indefinitely?"

"I'm not the right doctor to answer that question. Can I recommend we complete your physical evaluation? Then, you can begin therapy sessions as soon as your schedule will allow it." He steps back and takes a good look at my head. "Don't put it off," he adds. Grabbing my head and slightly tilting it to the side, he asks, "Now, tell me about this injury here."

He's looking at the gash I once had on my head from the plane crash. I try to explain everything to him as best I can. How it happened, what it felt like, what Guy said it looked like, how long the bleeding lasted, and how long I felt it took to heal.

"It would have been best for you to have stitches, of course," Dr. Braxton explains, "but under the circumstances, it healed very nicely. There's an ointment I can prescribe to reduce the scar."

I remember how Guy took care of all my wounds, including this one. He applied pressure on anything that bled, and even in the case of my head, he held my wound closed while I fell asleep from exhaustion. I didn't pick up on his chivalry at the time; I was too angry about too many things. But I came to learn his heart was surprisingly bigger than his mouth and temper.

"I probably would have died if it wasn't for Guy Harrington," I confess with a low voice. "He's the man who was lost and stranded with me."

With his head still very close to mine, the doctor listens while examining. "Yes, I know Mr. Harrington. He said the same thing about you."

"How is he?" I quickly ask. "How's his leg?"

The doctor gives me a gentle smile. "I can't discuss other patients. But I can tell you that you were lucky to have each other there."

I nod as he turns around to grab two latex gloves from what's shaped as a tissue box. "Since we're doing a full physical, I think it's a good idea to do a pap smear test."

"Okay," I quietly agree, leaning back and propping my legs up onto metal stirrups.

I really wish I weren't alone right now. I don't try to hold back my quiet tears from falling down my face.

A cold and harsh probe is pushed inside me. I can't help but think about how fucked up my expectations were. I thought I would be sitting here, getting an ultrasound to see the first picture of my baby. Instead, the uncomfortable feeling of metal is being shoved inside me.

"Hmm," the doctor says while examining me.

"What is it?" I ask, wiping away my tears.

He swipes a Q-tip inside me, making me tense. "When was your last pap?"

I can feel my eyes flutter, trying to think. "I-I can't remember. Not for a long time. My husband was the only man I had ever been with, so I didn't think it was necessary." I cringe, knowing that's not the case anymore.

"Well," he says, scooting back and loosening the metal equipment he stuck inside me, "you seem to have abnormal cervical discharge, which is likely the reason you haven't been able to get pregnant."

"What does that mean?" I ask, not knowing if I can handle any more bad news.

"I took a sample. It'll be analyzed, and we'll let you know the results in a day or two."

"Are you saying, I *can't* get pregnant?"

He calmly explains, "We don't know for sure until the lab results are back. But infertility is a possibility."

I sit up. "I can't take this. Please leave. I want to go home."

The doctor pushes his chair back and stands. He steps toward the door and pauses. "Mrs. Devereux, I realize this isn't what you expected. Under the circumstances and what you've been through, I'll put a rush on the lab work. We'll let you know the results as soon as possible."

I nod harshly, knowing that I'll lose my mind if I try to speak.

# Thirty-One

Leaving the outpatient building, I decide it's best to go home. Charles might be there, waiting for me. There are so many things I still need to apologize for and try to explain. I feel terrible for making him think that we were going to have a baby. I've probably hurt him with that misunderstanding as much as I've hurt myself. But then again, I could be wrong. He could be happy that I'm not pregnant. He doesn't have any reason not to leave me now. After what I did to betray his trust, I'm not sure if I would blame him.

And the possibility of being infertile … my stomach turns as I think about it.

I step toward the curb, thinking about taking a cab home, but I change my mind. I could use the time and space to clear my head. It's only about ten blocks.

Before the crash, I took a car everywhere I went. Walking seems more appealing to me now.

I unlock our front door and take one step into our home. One step is all I need to know he isn't here. The echo of my high heel on the marble floor is the only thing that fills the air. No signs of life.

"Charles," I call out for him, knowing he won't answer me.

I walk through every room, checking and making sure he hasn't holed himself up somewhere. I just need a sign that there is still hope, and him being in our home would give me that sign.

I find Kathy in our master bathroom. She startles me. Deep down, I really wasn't expecting to find anyone.

"Mrs. Devereux, I'm so sorry I scared you. Do you need me to draw you a bath, or do you need some privacy? I can finish cleaning this room later."

I take a deep sigh. "No, Kathy. Thank you for the offer. I was just looking for Charles."

She crinkles her brows and looks deep in thought. "You know, I don't think I've seen him at all today."

I nod. "I was afraid of that," I quietly say. "I think I'll go for a walk. If you do see Mr. Devereux, will you call me right away?"

"Yes, ma'am," Kathy agrees.

I can't decide if I want to cry or not. Walking alone on the Manhattan sidewalks makes me feel lonely. I'm surrounded by so many people, and I still can't get rid of this isolated feeling I have. My stomach rumbles, and I remember what Dr. Braxton told me.

*I need to remember to eat several small meals a day.*

My nose becomes warm, and I fight the urge to allow my tears to surface. A drink doesn't sound too bad either.

Rosette, my favorite French restaurant in the city, is only a few blocks away.

When I walk in, the hostess asks if Mr. Devereux will be joining me. I just shake my head and let her know I'll be sitting alone at the bar today.

Normally, I would want to enjoy a glass of champagne with a light meal, but today, I need something stronger. I order the fig and olive tapenade and two fingers, neat, of Glenmorangie, a twenty-five-year-old scotch whiskey. My father is a whiskey drinker on a daily basis. My mother drinks wine unless something is wrong. When her mother died, whiskey was what she reached for. It was her tell. How I knew she was going through something.

*Well, I'm going through something now.*

My fingers warm as I wrap them around the glass. I take a moment to admire the sight of the caramel-colored liquor, and then I place the glass under my nose and allow the scent to intoxicate me.

*And, now, for a taste.*

My lips hit the smooth glass, my eyes close, and my wrist tilts back. But before I get a sip, a hand comes and snatches the glass out of my hand and sets it down in front of me.

"What the hell do you think you're doing?" a deep voice says behind me.

Even with my eyes closed, I know who it is. I could smell his hand as soon as it was near me. His voice is the dead giveaway.

I open my eyes. "Guy, what are you doing here?"

Leaning against the bar between me and the barstool next to me, he looks around and to each side of where I'm sitting. "Are you here alone?" he asks.

"Answer my question first," I softly demand. "What are you doing here?"

He comes to some sort of conclusion and takes the seat closest to him, to my left.

I look around the restaurant, wondering who might see Guy sitting next to me. I suppose it doesn't matter. Charles has obviously gone home to his mother to sulk. She probably knows everything by now.

"I'm hungry," Guy explains. "And I love this restaurant. Remember?"

We argued over this restaurant. Over the head chef and his best dish. Or were we arguing over what his most popular dish was? They're not always one and the same.

I bite my lip, trying not to smile at the silliness of our disagreement. "Yes, I remember. Are you here alone?"

He moves his finger back and forth. "Uh-uh. No. I answered your question. Now, you need to answer mine. Why are you here alone, and why are you drinking? Are you crazy?"

My eyes avert down to my drink, now sitting on the solid countertop with Guy's arm lying in front of it. "I'm not pregnant," I tell him, not moving my gaze. I swallow hard. It hurts to say it again out loud. "And I told Charles about what happened between us." I turn my head toward Guy, tears teetering on my lower lids. "So, that's why I'm here alone." Then, I add a little too loudly, "And I might not ever be able to get pregnant."

Guy slowly breathes in, taking in what I just told him. He gestures to the bartender and requests the same drink.

"You're not alone," he tells me and places his hand on mine. "I'm sorry you're not pregnant. I know how badly you wanted it. I wanted that for you, too."

"It might not ever happen."

Guy shrugs. "You can always adopt."

The idea actually makes me smile, but then I think about how Gwendelyn would react.

*The Devereux bloodline*, I think dramatically to myself.

But I've always wanted to give a good life to children who might otherwise struggle.

Guy squeezes my hand, watching me think.

The warmth oozes into my skin and awakens my nerves. Memories and feelings of him touching me while we were on the island flood through me.

I try to ignore those feelings. Setting them aside, I pick up my glass. Guy joins me with his. I fight the urge of following tradition and make a point not to toast. We are not celebrating anything here. I only hold up my whiskey and nod in his direction before allowing the liquid to move down my throat, coaxing my insides with a numbing fire. The burn is laced with flavor.

I crave another. Removing my hand from under Guy's, I raise my finger at the bartender and gesture for another drink. Guy raises his and subtly tries to motion back and forth between the two of us, requesting another round for him as well.

"So, now, tell me, why aren't you with your wife?" I ask him, leaning on the bar, propping myself up with one elbow. "She looked really happy to see you when we got back."

His eyebrows animatedly move up and down. "Oh, she was." He smacks his lips. "She and the photogs she dragged behind her. It's her plan to hoist herself further into the limelight."

I sit up straight. "Hey, speaking of photogs." I nod to the bartender who just set our new round of whiskey in front of us. "What the hell happened? I understand that you sent the media over to our building to talk to us." I shake my head. "That was upsetting. We want nothing to do with the media." I take a sip. This round is more for savoring than shooting. "Under any circumstances, we don't welcome the attention."

Guy sips along with me. "I'm so sorry about that. I figured that was why your husband was trying to call."

"It *was* you," I accuse.

"Not exactly," he says. "You're not the only one who confessed to their spouse."

I place my hand over my mouth. "No," I say in shock. "I'm so sorry. That was a huge mistake for both of us, and I'm so, so sorry it's damaged your marriage, too."

"My marriage was already damaged."

"But she wanted to work it out."

"I don't," he snaps. "End of story." But his expression softens. "She knows it's over. She's just trying to blackmail me for a bigger piece of the pie in our divorce settlement."

"What is she threatening you with?"

"You," he simply says and turns to bore his eyes into me. "I told her to leave you alone. She sent the press your way to send me a message that she'll expose our affair if I don't give her more in the settlement."

A chill runs down my spine.

"Oh fuck," I exhale. My elbows slam on the counter in front of me, and my hands move up to the sides of my head and interlock in the back. "That is the last thing I need. It will be impossible for Charles to forgive me if this goes public. How could Marina do this? It's so heartless."

"Nay, it'll be fine." He uses a soothing voice. "I won't let her have my money, but I promise, I'll take care of it. I won't let her hurt you either."

I snap my head up and pound my fist on the counter. "No, it won't be fine. Charles left me. Or at least, he will for sure once I tell him we might not ever be able to conceive." My words have a heavy weight and bring a startling realization.

I begin to cry, and Guy immediately stands and holds on to me from behind. He's cradling me and comforting me with his embrace. Even after I saw the hurt on his face in the newspaper photo, he genuinely feels sorry for me.

"I don't even know what to do or where to go," I sob. "I don't even know who I am without him."

"Hey," he says, prompting me to sit more upright and look at him. His finger goes under my chin, and he keeps his face so close to mine that I can taste the whiskey on his breath. "I know exactly who you are. You're a strong, feisty, beautiful survivor."

When his finger moves from my chin, I look away. "No. You're the survivor. I wouldn't have made it off the plane if it wasn't for you. I wouldn't have made it through that storm on the raft if it wasn't for you, and I know I wouldn't have been able to survive on that island for over a month if it wasn't for you."

He uses the pad of his thumb to wipe a tear from under my eye. "I wouldn't have wanted to get off that sinking plane if it wasn't for you."

I laugh, almost spitting out my drink. "You're so full of it. You didn't even know me. And," I add, "you hated me when you first met me."

He breathes in a deep and controlled breath. "No, I was having a bad day, and you frustrated me."

I know what he's talking about. He was physically attracted to me from the moment he saw me. As much as I'd love to deny it, there's no point. We were instantly attracted to each other.

"It was just you who hated me," he says and coolly takes a final sip of his whiskey.

I tip my glass back and finish mine, giving me liquid courage and a burn that feels so good right now. "Wrong. You frustrated me, too, and I didn't know how to handle it," I admit.

Guy slides a credit card over the bar top, and the bartender swipes it right away.

"I know where we can find much better whiskey than this." He turns to the bartender and adds, "No offense."

The man just shrugs, seeming not to care about Guy's statement.

Guy's eyes return to me, and he stands up straight, offering his hand. "Will you come with me?" he asks.

That's an awfully big request for a day like today. But I've got no place else to be and nobody else to be with.

After glancing at the new phone Charles gave me yesterday and seeing that I haven't missed a call, I take Guy's hand.

"Yes," I tell him, and I let him take me out of the restaurant.

# Thirty-Two

Guy walks me past his doorman and tells him I'm allowed up to his penthouse anytime, any hour.

I nervously tell him, "That's not necessary."

"I just want you to know I'm always here if you need me. You never have to think twice about it," he says as we walk toward the elevator. "Watch," he instructs. "Here's the code to get to my floor."

I look down at his fingers pressing four buttons, but I let him know, "I don't need to know that. I'm just coming up for a drink; that's all." I lean my head against the elevator wall as it goes up. "What about your wife? She's not here?"

He shakes his head as if my question is absurd. "Marina has been at The Plaza since I've been back. She'll be there until we settle on our divorce terms. Unfortunately, she likes to pop in every now and then to argue."

"So, she might show up?" I ask nervously.

Guy grins, staring at me. His mind is obviously somewhere else. "The doorman will give me a heads-up," he says as the elevator doors open.

As soon as I take one step inside Guy's modern Fifth Avenue apartment, I immediately feel guilty. "This is a mistake," I tell him. "I shouldn't be here."

"It's just me, Nay," he reassures me. "We shouldn't have to go from only having each other to never being allowed alone together."

I pull out my phone and look at the screen again. Charles still hasn't called, and Kathy hasn't called to tell me he's home. I don't have any indication that he's looking for me. *What does it matter where I get my whiskey?*

I look around, and I'm drawn toward the floor-to-ceiling windows overlooking the downtown skyline.

"It's a great view."

It's beautiful, lit up at night.

He nods while pouring our drinks from a nearby console. "It's not the park, but I like it. There's history in the skyline."

His thoughts on our city make me smile. People are usually drawn to the excitement and money found in Manhattan, but it's rich with history and milestones, too.

Guy hands me two fingers of warm liquid. The smell alone is intoxicating. But not as intoxicating as the scent of Guy himself.

He bends down, searching for my eyes, which I'm trying to hide from him. "Nay, I really am sorry about the baby. I still know that you're going to be a great mother someday. Even if it's not the way you thought it would be."

I bring my head up. "I don't know what's going to happen."

It wouldn't have even been his baby, and he was ready to raise it and protect it with me just because it was mine.

"That's all part of the adventure," he says.

We keep staring at each other a little too long until I finally look away.

"Have you looked at our island on satellite?" he asks as I scuff my feet along his living room floor, keeping my eye on the view.

I shake my head and smile at Guy's playfulness. It seems like such a trivial thing to do. We lived on it. Why do I need to see what it looks like from space?

He brings his phone screen over to me. "See? There." He moves his thumb and pointer finger further apart on the screen and zooms in. "That's our island."

I can see the opening in the trees that exposes the pool we used to bathe and swim in. That was my favorite feature of the island. I remember the first time I touched myself, the first time I saw the masculinity of Guy's naked body, and the flat boulder we first had sex on. Or *fucked* on. I don't know what to call it anymore.

"That's not an island; it's a pimple," I observe.

Guy chuckles a little at my observation. "You're right. It hasn't even been named. What do you think about Nay-Guy?"

I laugh out loud. "You can't be serious."

"Guy-omi?" He tries to humor me.

Continuing to laugh, I manage to say, "Maybe that one is better."

Oh, it feels good to laugh and feel like I can freely be myself again. I've been under so much stress since we've been back.

His thumb moves back over his phone, and music begins to play throughout the apartment. He begins to sway, and I notice my body starts moving back and forth along with his.

"Dance with me?" he asks, holding out one hand.

Suddenly, I'm feeling shy again. "Guy, I don't know."

"Come on." He steps closer and takes the tumbler glass out of my hand, setting it on a nearby table.

I just let it happen. Before I know it, I'm holding his hand, and his other is wrapped around my waist. I'm moving back and forth with him. It feels as natural here as it did on the island.

"It's just a dance. I just want to be close," he whispers into my ear. His voice is calm and subtle so as not to scare me away.

I breathe him in, and the familiar scent brings back a comfort I forgot had soothed me. I'm confused as to why it doesn't actually feel wrong to be back in his arms. I need to be stronger than this.

"It was just six weeks," I whisper back as we move together. "We never should have cheated."

My body begins to tingle at the memory. I'm not sure if I'm in pain because of the guilt or because of the desire I'm holding back.

I pull my head back, but his doesn't move. Our mouths are only an inch apart.

"We're not on the island anymore," I breathe out onto his lips. "We can't do this."

The muscles between my legs begin to throb. My words say one thing, but my body reacts another way. My heartbeat feels as if it was spreading through my whole body, and I can feel it pumping and beating everywhere. Too much moisture collects in my mouth. I swallow and push it down, hoping it'll help cool my insides.

I can't stop focusing on his lips, knowing his tongue is hiding, wet behind them. I'm so hungry for it.

I shake my head and try to snap myself out of it.

Breathing heavy, I tell him, "I can't do this."

"I've heard that before, Nay." He's quick to raise his voice and take a small step away from me.

"Well, it's true," I argue back. "This is so … it's so …" *Wrong*. I think the word I'm looking for is *wrong*, but I can't seem to spit anything out.

"We might not be on the island, but you can't deny that this"—he moves his hand back and forth between us—"is still there."

"No," I lie to him and myself.

He grabs my hand and forces it down between his legs, making me feel his bulging mass. It makes me yearn for him even more. My lips quiver, but I stay silent and stunned, staring at him.

"It's here. I know what this does to you." He moves my hand up onto his chest, over his heart. "And it's here. I know what this does to you, too."

He reaches for me, sprawling his hands all over my body, like they're a weapon I'm powerless to.

"We have everything right here between us," he says huskily near my ear.

I try to step back and out of his reach, but I am actually powerless to his touch. I begin to breathe heavier, trying to fight this overwhelming urge I feel for him to be inside me.

"It's here for you, too, isn't it?" he asks as he spreads his hands over my chest, moving his fingers over each breast.

His hands move to the back of my neck, making my head instinctively cock back, opening my mouth. And I want him to kiss me. But his hands don't stop moving until they run down my back, cup my ass, and reach between my legs where his fingers graze over my clit.

"Here," he says into my open mouth.

My knees feel weak, and my core quakes from too much anticipation. He takes my hand and cups my fingers around my sex as he moves his hand over them, making me massage myself.

"What we have between us isn't just me. This is for you, too. This is who you are, and this is what we are together."

I stop fighting him, and I move my hand, just like he wants.

"Ah," I mewl out one little sound, and it completely unglues both of us.

I'm panting, wanting to inhale him, as he grabs my face and pulls our mouths together. I miss the way he tastes. I can still smell the salt water misting in the air, and when my eyes are closed, I can hear waves crashing on the shore behind us.

"I want you, Nay. I'm not going to apologize for it," he speaks into my mouth. "I want your mind, body, and soul."

Our tongues continue to move around each other, trying to lap up as much as we possibly can. He brings his hand down and goes under my skirt to run his fingers around the rim of my underwear.

"Oh," I can't help but cry out.

"Tell me you want me," he says, taking his thumb and pushing it inside me.

"Oh," I say again. "I want you," I cry out, needing so much more.

He unbuttons his pants and pulls down his briefs just enough for his cock to be let free. It's just how I remembered it. Less than a week ago, it belonged all to me, and now, I need to have it again as soon as possible.

I grab on to his face, pulling his body close enough to me to feel his hard cock against me. He grabs my skirt and hoists it up, so the bottom hem is over my hips. Still kissing me, he takes both hands down to my panties and rips them apart, allowing the pieces to fall to the floor.

Grabbing my right hip and pulling it up, he takes two steps forward until my ass hits the cold glass window. His dick shoves right into my opening. He goes in deep and urgent, holding it in for a second. Even his kiss stills as he takes in the first contact.

"Yes!" I breathlessly say.

Finally, I'm getting what I want. I've been craving it longer than I care to admit. At this moment, I hope he never leaves from inside me. He fills me in more places than I thought possible.

He begins to move, making me call out every time he goes back in and hits my far back walls. Each time he repeats his movements, it's just as good as the first.

The sensation of the cold glass on my back and the warm movement I feel in my body is amazing. I've never felt so alive.

His mouth moves to my neck, and I arch back, wanting to give him as much skin as I can. When his hands move down to around my ass, I instinctively pick my legs up while he's still inside me. Crossing my ankles together at the small of his back, I hold myself on to him as he moves across the room and carries me to his bedroom.

When he sets me down, his cock slides out of me, and I suddenly feel empty without it. My desperate panting tells him he can't stop now.

"I told you I wanted you. I want to savor you," he tells me, stepping into me, forcing me to sit down on the bed behind me. "I need to see your body again." He leans forward and pulls my skirt down under my ass and off my legs. Tossing it behind him, he grins to find my exposed lower half in front of him. "I've missed your naked body."

His eyes become more serious and predatory as he leans over me. Taking his right hand up to my chest, he begins to unbutton my blouse, one button at a time. His other hand runs between my legs.

"You've shaved," he observes and places one finger inside me. "Civilization looks good on you."

What we're doing is anything but civilized. This is pure animal instinct.

I reach up and start unbuttoning his shirt at the same pace he continues to unbutton my blouse. When I'm done, he violently shrugs his dress shirt off his shoulders and throws my blouse open. I sit up on my elbows, and he grabs my bra, throwing it over my head and forcing me to put my arms in the air. Before I can even bring them down, he's got his arm wrapped around my back, pressing our skin together.

He crawls across the bed, carrying me under him, until we hit the headboard. Finally, I feel his cock back inside me. The void I was missing for the past sixty seconds has been filled again.

"I want to fuck you all night, Naomi," he tells me while I watch his abs flex as he moves back and forth inside me. My body responds to his deep, gruff voice. "Tell me you want it, Nay."

Faster than I can think, I yell out, "I want it, Guy. I want you to keep fucking me. I love it when you're inside me." I thrust my hips up, showing him just how much I want it—hard and deep.

Maybe it's because I'm not thinking, but I've never spoken like that before. It's as if my mouth and body are acting without me.

I can feel the heat rising all over my skin, and our bodies both begin to glisten. It's just like we're still on the island, except this bed is softer and more comfortable. I'm more at ease with the mattress on my back instead of a rock or sand. I can't believe it, but the sex is even better.

My insides feel as if they're building pressure.

"I can feel you, Nay. You want to come. Tell me you want to come."

I toss my head back. "Oh God, I want to come so bad. Make me come, Guy." I feel as if I would kill for my orgasm right now. I'd do anything.

"Yes, baby," he answers my call.

He speeds up his pace with a fast, steady rhythm, making me continue to scream out his name, begging him to take it just a little further over my tipping point. Just a little more.

His thumb moves over my clit, and—*pow*. The pleasure is so deep and so penetrating. If it wasn't for the euphoria spreading through me, I could mistake the intensity for pain. He continues to move inside me and rub his finger over my nub but at a slower rate until it's a rolling, smooth motion.

I can feel him spasming and releasing himself inside me until he shoves one last thrust and holds himself in me, allowing everything he has to drain inside my body.

The heartbeat I feel throughout my whole body begins to slow, and I feel more labored and tired. Guy falls on top of me and rolls us to our side. My head goes limp on the pillow, but Guy continues to consume me by kissing my neck.

I love how everything is slowing down, but the touch and sensations are still there, and they're not done yet.

"Stay with me tonight," he whispers in my ear. "Don't take your body away from me. There's so much more I want to do. So many things I want to say."

Reality hits, and my eyes pop open wide. I sit up and bury my head in my hands. "Why am I so confused? It's not supposed to be like this. This isn't me."

Guy sits up and leans forward to kiss my back. "This is you. Charles doesn't know you like I know you."

The mention of my husband makes something inside me snap.

# Thirty-Three

I abruptly stand up. "I can't stay here. Oh fuck. We shouldn't have done this. I shouldn't have done this." I continue to ramble, "This was a mistake. I have to go home. What am I doing?"

"You don't have to go anywhere," Guy says, watching me, worried, as I frantically grab my clothes.

"Yes, I do. I'm married, and I care about my husband." I look around, searching for something. "And where is my fucking underwear?"

Guy jumps to his feet. "I love you, Nay!" he screams at me. "He left you alone today. I love you. And I'm pretty sure you love me, too."

"You don't love me. You love fucking me!" I scream so uncontrollably that I drop all the clothes in my hand. Bending down to gather them again, I'm much calmer. "And Charles left me because of it. Or maybe he didn't. Maybe he'll come back," I begin to mumble to myself, trying to convince myself that it'll all be okay.

But there is only one way there will ever be a chance for things to be okay again.

I snap up and pointedly stare at Guy. "We can't ever see each other again."

"Bullshit," he spits, standing there in front of me, naked, with his hands on his hips. "This isn't done. *We* are not done."

I shove past him with my shoulder and leave his bedroom. "Of course it's done. We never even started. We're not on the island anymore. This is reality," I say, knowing he's following me. "There's no place for you and me here."

Guy catches up to me in his living room. "This is more real"—he reaches out and grabs my left wrist, pulling my arm out and making my clothes fall to the floor again—"than this shit." He holds up my hand for us to both notice the unavoidable rock on my finger.

I snatch my hand back. "It's the only thing that's real."

"You're full of shit, Nay, and you know it. You're just fooling yourself, but you don't fool me."

*There they are*. I finally spot my underwear.

"Damn it," I say, holding up the scraps of my thong. I shake my head and throw them back on the ground. I pick up my clothes, one piece at a time, and get dressed without my underwear.

"You can be with me," he says, still naked, just staring at me as I dress.

"No," I quickly retort.

He's visibly frustrated. His hand goes up and pulls at his jaw. "I love you, Nay. You can be with me."

"No," I say again. "You're not my husband."

Once I'm dressed, I march back into his bedroom. I don't bother to tuck in my blouse or straighten my skirt. I grab my heels and storm out with them in my hand. My purse is on a table by the front door. I pick it up and shove it under my armpit as I swing the door open.

"Naomi, don't leave," Guy begs behind me.

I don't answer. I just keep moving forward until I'm in the middle of the hallway. I can hear Guy's footsteps behind me.

"Naomi," he calls out to me one more time.

I stop and turn to see the most perfect-looking, unashamed, naked man standing in the middle of a hallway in an upscale building, yelling my name.

"I'm sorry," is all I can say to him.

He looks as if I punched him in the stomach.

"I'm so, so sorry," I say even softer, wanting to be gentle. "I can own up to what we did on the island, but I can't justify what we just did tonight. I don't know why I did it. All I know is that it was wrong, and I'm supposed to be with Charles."

Guy stands there still, not moving and not reacting. I take in one last look at his virile body before I turn around and walk away from him.

Once the doors close in the elevator, I put my shoes on. When I bend over to slide them on my feet, a tear falls down.

*Enough of that*, I tell myself and wipe the tear away. *You're doing the right thing.*

When the doors open, I'm ready to leave and forget about this whole night. I need to be home, waiting for Charles to come back to me. As impossible as it feels, I need to expel all thoughts of Guy.

I can hear the blatant echoes of my shoes tapping on the tiled floor of his lobby. I don't pick my head up until I hear that my echoes are not alone. There are other high heels marching their way toward me.

When I look up, I'm face-to-face with Marina. My walk slows, and hers does, too, when we pass each other. I swallow hard, pushing my nerves down my throat. She just glares at me, and it's obvious she knows who I am and where I just came from. By the looks of my disheveled hair and clothing, I'm sure she can imagine what I was doing in her husband's apartment.

I can see the doorman frantically making a phone call in the corner of my eye. I try to keep my dignity in tact, keeping my head forward and focused on leaving the building, but I can feel Marina's head turn and watch me as I walk to the doors to exit. Guy has more to deal with than me leaving.

He's going to have to face his own spouse and the remains of their marriage.

*What have I done?*

I might live with the guilt for the rest of my life. And Guy … I broke his heart. I can't believe he thinks his love for me is real. He's just confused because sex ruins and complicates everything. I never wanted to hurt him.

"Naomi," her voice calls behind me.

I stop in my tracks, staring at the French doors I need to go through to exit. But it's too late. She knows I heard her.

I turn around and pull my purse higher on my shoulder, trying to appear more dignified than I feel.

She steps closer to me while I stand still. "I can't believe you're still sleeping with my husband."

Just as I open my mouth to make some silly, unjustified excuse, the elevator doors open, and Guy comes running out, barefoot and bare-chested, with only a pair of jeans on.

*Oh no, this isn't good.*

"Naomi, wait!" He runs right past Marina but stops when he's close enough to see the humiliation on my face. He barely glances at Marina. "Don't worry about her. She means nothing to me."

"Guy, how can you say that?" Marina squeals.

"Look," he says, staring into my eyes, "you're still the only woman in the world who matters to me. She just wants more money now that I'm back. I just want *you*."

Marina places her hand on his arm. "My lawyers will have a field day with this."

"I don't care," he snaps and yanks his arm free. "Go weave whatever publicity stunt you want. I choose Naomi."

Marina grabs her phone and turns away from Guy, mumbling, "You're gonna regret that."

But Guy ignores her. He reaches down and takes my hand. "Nay, I choose you whether you choose me or not. Being on the island changed me. It made me a better man who won't take anything for granted. I want to be this better man with you."

It's hard to look him in the eye, so I look down. This is so much more painful than I could have imagined.

*Why won't my feet move? Why can't I walk away right now?*

"I choose you. Will you choose me?" He steps closer, and our foreheads touch. "You can't leave me because, if you leave, that's it. If you go back and ask Charles for forgiveness, you and I are done. I won't let you back in if he doesn't forgive you. I need to know that you're choosing me because you love me, too, not because I'm your only option, like I was on the island."

I pull back and look into his eyes. "What if I do love you, too, but I still can't choose you?"

"Yes, you can." He chokes up as I take a step back.

I take another step backward before saying a final, "I can't," and I turn around to walk out the doors.

This time, he doesn't follow me out. And that hurts.

My hand flies up, and a cab immediately pulls over. Before I pull open the door to get in, I think about what I'm doing. I love Charles, but I think I love Guy, too. I want to stay, but I know it's not the right thing to do.

With my heart pulling me in the other direction, I open the door and get into the cab. When it begins to drive away, that's when I feel my heart break.

I turn in my seat and see him stepping outside his building. Our eyes meet and remain locked on each other until he's out of sight.

*Why does this feel wrong? It shouldn't. I should feel like I'm doing the right thing by leaving him.*

It's past ten when I get into my building. Kathy is in her quarters, and the deafening silence when I walk in the door tells me I'm alone. Charles still hasn't come back.

I've lost them both.

I want to breathe in the mahogany and antique smell of our apartment that I love so much, but all I can smell is Guy. His masculine scent is still lingering on me, my clothes, and my body. I start stripping on my way to the master bedroom.

I'm about to throw my clothes in the dry cleaning hamper, but I stop. *I can't keep these.*

Instead, I walk across the hall and toss them in the utility room trash, expelling them forever.

It's cold when I step into the shower. I didn't want to wait for the water to warm up, but it does quickly. It reminds me of how the cold glass felt on my ass when Guy's warm dick was inside me.

I stomp my foot and pound my fist on the tiled wall in front of me. I can't think about that anymore. I can never think about Guy again. I need to remove him from my brain.

When I wash my hair and massage my head, I visualize my fingers drawing out the memory of Guy. It's soothing, and it might be working.

By the time I step out of the shower, I feel a little more refreshed. I scrunch the towel around my hair before I wrap the towel around my body.

I breathe in deep and hold the scent in my lungs before slowly letting it out. Lavender soap. I've washed Guy off of me. Now, I'm wearing the scent Charles brought home for me six months ago.

"Just because," he said.

It wasn't uncommon for him to surprise me with little gifts out of the blue. He's a good man and a good husband, and he doesn't deserve what I did to him.

With my towel still wrapped around my body, I leave the bathroom for the bedroom where I left my phone on the nightstand. It's a long shot, but I have to know if he's tried to call me.

I gasp as soon as I enter the room.

# Thirty-Four

"You're here. You're really here."

Charles is sitting on the edge of the bed, facing the bathroom. He must have been waiting for me to get out of the shower. I practically run to be by his side. Sliding down to my knees in front of him, I throw my face in his lap and begin to cry.

"Forgive me. Please forgive me," I beg.

He doesn't react.

Eventually, he picks up his hand and begins to pet my hair as I still lie with my face buried in his lap.

"I want to be so mad at you," he says, still touching my wet hair. His voice begins to tremble when he repeats, "I want to be so mad. But I missed you so much."

My head picks up. "Charles, do you know that I love you?"

He nods before changing his mind and shaking his head. "I just don't understand it. I couldn't stop thinking about you while you were gone. I thought about you every second of every day. How could you have forgotten about me so fast?"

"I never forgot about you," I say as I rise up to sit next to him on the bed. "All I wanted was to be back home where I belonged. I never wanted to be on that island."

His head hangs down. "Then, why did you do it?" he asks.

*Because my body made me—and maybe my heart, too.*

My hand goes to his leg, and I speak to him even though he can't look at me, "Because I lost my mind. Uh …" I try to think of a reasonable excuse. "Maybe it was a coping mechanism for me to believe that I was never going to be rescued. I got to a point where I couldn't go on with being afraid and disappointed that no one was ever going to find us."

I lie to my husband, but I can't help but remember how Guy always saw right through my bullshit. He instantly knew me better than I knew myself.

Charles flinches at the mention of *us*. "You're attracted to him." His statement jars me, as I know it must hurt him to think of it.

*Yes*, my body wants to scream, still throbbing from being with Guy earlier, but my mind tells it to shut up.

"Honey, it wasn't about that. Bonding with him … it was this crazy instinct I had for survival. That's all it was."

"Oh, come on, Naomi. I might be a heterosexual man, but I'm not stupid. I'm nothing compared to Guy Harrington." The defeat in his voice breaks my heart.

I don't have to lie to him this time when I say, "You're the most generous, kindhearted man I've ever known, and I don't deserve you. I know I don't deserve your forgiveness either, but I'd like to ask for it anyway."

He nods slowly but still seems unsure, and then he looks away from me again. "There isn't still some small part of you that's attracted to him? Some small part of you that still wants him in that way?"

I don't think I can continue lying. I don't want to have to lie for the rest of my life, so I ignore his question. I just need to know one thing. "Do you think you could ever forgive me?"

Charles takes a deep breath through his nose. "I have to," he answers. "You're my best friend. I've never felt angry like this with you. We've never even fought before." He takes another deep breath and nods to himself. "I'm still hurt, but I forgive you."

"You forgive me?" I ask Charles, almost in disbelief.

He nods. "I'll try."

His arm reaches over and lifts up my left hand. He rubs his thumb over my ring. "You never took it off?" he asks.

I shake my head. "No."

When he brings his head up and turns to me, I finally feel like we have eye contact. There's my husband, my best friend and companion, behind those eyes. I feel as if we're on the verge of a breakthrough in this major betrayal I've caused in our marriage.

"I can forgive you," he states clearly.

It's what I've been waiting to hear, what I've wanted, but I feel like I'm now betraying myself.

"As long," he continues, "as you promise me"—his face becomes serious and concerned, and a wrinkle above his nose tells me he's deep in thought, considering his words—"that it was just on the island. It's in the past, and it has nothing to do with the life we have together. You and I will go back to life the way we were before you were lost. The way we've always been."

His hand moves up, and he rubs the pad of his thumb in the middle of my forehead. I breathe in, slow and serene, savoring the comfort this simple gesture of affection gives me. Then, I feel his lips lightly press on my forehead, and I know everything will be okay if I just promise him what he wants to hear.

But I can't. I can't lie to him anymore either.

"But I've changed, Charles. I can't go back to being the same person I was."

"It was only six weeks. How could you have changed?"

It would be hard to explain it to someone who didn't experience it with me. I try anyway. "I just feel different. I'm stronger. I want to laugh more, be spontaneous, adventurous, fight more."

Charles looks confused and surprised. "Why on earth would you want to fight with your husband?"

I smile a little, thinking about my silly banter with Guy. "Because it's okay to be bold and disagree. It's okay to be passionate."

"That's ridiculous. We've never been a couple who argues."

I stand up and face him. "We're arguing now."

"What has gotten into you, Naomi? I forgive you. Why can't we go back to the way things were?"

I shake my head and let a sorrowful tear fall. "Because I'm not the same woman anymore. I'm so sorry, Charles. We both deserve more than a platonic marriage."

He looks at me, concerned. "But what if that's what I want? Shouldn't what I want matter?"

"Yes, but I want more for you, Charles. I want more for me, too."

He bows his head and runs his hands over his bald scalp. "What the hell did that guy do to you on that island? Where is my wife?"

"You don't know him," I calmly say.

"Look," Charles hastily says, "I'm tired. I didn't sleep last night. Let's just get some rest and talk about this in the morning."

I nod and move to my side of the bed. "Where were you last night? Did you go to your mother's?" The thought makes me sad, knowing the things Gwendelyn must have said about me.

"No," he rasps, laying his head down. "I checked into a hotel for the night. After you said you were pregnant, I didn't want Mother to know we were having problems."

My stomach turns, as I know there's so much more I need to tell him.

"Charles," I say quietly.

"In the morning, Naomi. Right now, I want to sleep and pretend like everything is back to normal."

I know I must be tired, but my eyes won't close.

For hours, I lie with my eyes open, wondering if Guy was right. I've changed, and Charles doesn't know me like Guy now knows me.

Just as my eyelids start to close, Charles stirs and sleepily lays his hand on my side. I look down at where his hand is and realize that I feel nothing—no tingles, no excitement, nothing. I never did feel anything when he touched me, not even before the plane crash.

When I wake up, I find Charles shaving in our master bathroom.

"I let you sleep in," he says as he moves the razor up his jawline.

I turn my phone over in my hand, so I can see the time. It's almost ten a.m., and there's a voice message. I read the transcript:

Mrs. Devereux, this is Dr. Braxton. Your lab results are in, and I'm sorry to say that your abnormal cervical mucus is hostile, which means it is thick and makes it unlikely for sperm to get through for fertilization. There are hormonal treatments we can discuss, or I can refer you to a fertility specialist.

I can hear the scraping sound of Charles's razor against his stubble.

"After you left the doctor's office yesterday, he did an exam. It will be very hard for me to get pregnant," I say quietly.

Charles freezes and slowly moves his gaze over his shoulder to me. He looks sorrowful, closing his eyes and breathing in.

"We can adopt," I suggest.

When he opens his eyes, he nods. "But Mother can't know. Maybe we'll go to Europe for a year and come home with an infant. I don't know. We'll figure it out."

I shake my head. "I don't want to hide an adoption. I certainly don't want to lie to a child while we raise him or her. And I don't understand why you would care what your mother thinks."

"It's not just Mother; it's our name. It's our—"

"Bloodline," I answer for him, feeling disappointed and disconnected from my husband.

He nods and goes back to facing the mirror, continuing to shave the other side of his face.

"Charles, we need to talk." I realize how very far apart we are on so many things now.

He continues to stare into the mirror. "About what?"

My mouth gapes open. "About the fact that I was in a plane crash, how I washed up on a deserted island, that I was scared but strong, and how I slept with someone else."

He sets his razor down but continues to stare at his reflection. "I told you, I want things to go back to the way things were. I don't want to talk about anything that happened to you while you were gone." He takes a breath before raising his voice. "And I certainly don't want to talk about Guy Harrington. Yesterday, I asked Henry to find information on him. Do you know you're not the first one he has used to cheat on his poor wife with?"

"You don't"—I swallow hard, struggling to control my emotions—"know the whole story."

"Once a cheater, always a cheater."

I breathe hard, trying not to yell. "That's not what this is," bursts out of my mouth, and I immediately shut it when I see the look on Charles's face.

"This?" he questions. "What do you mean, that's not what *this* is?"

I swallow hard and try to feel brave. "I would have died without him. He would have died without me. We needed each other to survive. There's a bond between us that I don't think I can explain. It's—"

"Stronger than marriage?" he snaps at me. "We have a bond, in matrimony."

I take a deep breath, and then I let it out. "I'm in love with him," I confess, surprising even myself.

"You're not in love with him, Naomi. You're confused. Sex complicates things. You and I don't need to base our relationship on sex. There is history, friendship, and I thought respect. Now, you've gone and thrown it all away because you couldn't handle being alone long enough for me to have you rescued."

"It wasn't like that," I grunt out. I can't pretend what he said doesn't hurt.

"Wasn't it?" he yells, making me flinch.

I stand up and face him. "There's no passion between us, Charles."

"This is a marriage."

And, now, the room is full of silence so thick, you could cut through the air between us.

"Exactly," I say calmly. "I'm your wife, and we don't touch each other unless we're trying to make a baby. We might not even have that anymore. Do you even enjoy having sex with me?"

Charles scoffs and puts his hands on his hips.

"I love everything we have, but I want more. I want more for you, too."

He nods and averts his eyes away from me. I can see the hurt I've caused all over his face.

"You're right; you have changed. You're not the woman I married."

"I'm not," I agree. "I didn't ask for what happened to me, nor did I cause it. But it has changed me, and I'm not ashamed of it—not anymore."

I can almost see the energy leaving his body. He falls to his knees and hangs his head in front of me. "Why are you doing this?"

I step into him, closer so that his head rests on my stomach. My hand runs over his smooth head, and I let him sob against me.

"I'm so sorry," I whisper down to him as I take off my engagement ring. "I don't think we belong together after all."

# Thirty-Five

Nearly an hour went by with Charles crying and me embracing him, mourning the loss of our marriage. But I knew I had to let go. Charles knew he needed to let go, too.

The only thing I said before I left was about how truly sorry I was and how badly I wanted him to be happy. I meant it. I want him to find the same kind of passion that I know I've found with Guy.

I never would have found the real person I was deep down if it wasn't for Guy and the relationship we developed on the island. If I had met him in Manhattan, nothing would have ever happened between us. It never could have gotten that far. It was the island that brought out the best in me, the best in him, and it brought us together.

It feels refreshing to step out of my and Charles's apartment building and into the crisp air alone and without the heavy weight of guilt, knowing I made a choice for myself. Not because it was the right thing to do, but because it was what my heart had told me to do.

I want to go straight to Guy's apartment, but I'm not sure if he'll even want me again after I left him. But I've got to try. He needs to know that I do choose him and what we have isn't just in the past.

It doesn't take long for me to find a cab and get to Guy's apartment building.

When I get to the elevator, I punch in the same code he used earlier and wait while it takes me to the top floor.

I practically jog down the hallway to his unit and anxiously knock on his door. I'm feeling hopeful and excited to see him.

But my face drops when the door opens, and my heart feels like it falls into my stomach.

"Marina, I need to talk to Guy."

She leans against the doorframe, crossing her arms in front of her. "Apparently, he doesn't care if he lives here or not."

"Where is he?"

She tilts her head, curiously looking at me. "I don't know." She shrugs. "The Plaza, The Ritz-Carlton. For all I care, he's on the moon."

I take a step back, ready to go find him. But curiosity gets the better of me. "Why are you here? Why isn't he here?"

"Because he finally found something he loves more than money. You," she explains. "He agreed to all my terms in the settlement, even this apartment. Our lawyers will iron it out tomorrow."

"Why would he do that?"

Marina only looks slightly ashamed of herself. "Because I threatened to go public with the affair you had on the island. But he didn't even put up a fight this time. I think you broke him."

"I need his cell number," I ask urgently.

She gives me a snide look. "Good luck with that."

I inhale sharply, and I use language I never in my life thought I would be able to use. "Fuck you, you greedy bitch."

I don't even wait for a response. I just turn and start for the elevator.

Downstairs, the doorman, who always seems to be on his damn phone, holds the door as I dash out, barely getting a, "Thank you," out as I pass him.

My hand flies up, and I wonder how I'm going to find Guy. The fact that I don't even know where to start barely enters my mind.

I grab a cab and remember what Marina mentioned. "The Plaza," I tell the driver.

The car barely slows when I swing the door open outside the grand hotel. I throw a twenty at the driver and run up the red-carpeted steps, so I can make my way into the hotel lobby. I head straight for a house phone next to the concierge stand.

"Connect me to Mr. Harrington's room. Guy Harrington," I say as soon as the operator picks up.

After a moment, she says, "I'm sorry. We don't have a Guy Harrington staying with us."

"Damn it." I hang up the phone and leave the hotel just as quickly as I entered.

When I get to the curb, I raise my arm to catch another taxi. Two headlights pull up to the front of the hotel right away. I swing the car door open, and I'm about to step into the backseat of the cab when someone grabs my arm from behind.

"Where do you think you're going?"

I keep my back to him and close my eyes, feeling the rush of adrenaline I get when we touch.

His other arm reaches past me and shuts the cab door. He taps the top of the car, letting the driver know he can leave without a passenger.

I turn slowly, savoring this moment, knowing that I'm with him again.

"I asked you a question. Where do you think you're going?" he repeats.

I almost laugh when I say, "The Ritz, the moon maybe." My arms slap down to my sides as I realize how crazed and ridiculous I was being. "I don't really know," I admit, looking down and laughing at myself. "I was just trying to find you. Even if you were on the moon."

"Well, you've found me." His tone is dry. Guy's hand reaches out, and the pad of his thumb runs across my jawline. He forces me to look at him. "I would never leave this island without you."

He could have mindlessly continued to touch me, but something holds him back. He drops his hand, and my smile falls with it.

"I told you, Nay, you had to choose me. I'm sorry Charles didn't forgive you, but I'm too far gone in love with you to settle for being your backup."

"You're not my backup. I went to your apartment, and Marina told me you gave her everything she wanted in the settlement."

His gray eyes look hurt and soft as they look into mine, but he's trying to be strong.

"I know," he admits. "I know you were at my apartment. I told Clyde, my doorman, to call me if he ever saw you."

"Why would you do that if you thought I chose Charles over you?"

He solemnly shrugs. "Because I needed to know. Naomi, why were you there?"

I look down, wanting to expel this distance I feel between us. I look back, staring right into him, and I can see it. He loves me.

"Call me Nay. I like when you call me Nay. You're the only one who has ever called me that."

He only stares back at me. He's guarded.

"Marina said you might be staying here, but the hotel didn't have your name. I was ready to go to every hotel in the city to find you."

Guy looks unsure. "I checked in under an alias, so Marina or her lawyers couldn't find me. We've said all we needed to say."

"You gave up your apartment, summer house, money—everything you've been fighting to hold on to—all for me? Even after you thought I didn't want you?"

"I still want to protect you." He looks down. "I chose you even if you didn't choose me. I'll choose you every time over everything. But I won't succumb myself to be with you if I don't have all of you."

I take a step closer to him, forcing him to look at me again. "Charles *did* forgive me."

His eyes spring open wider, and his hands run along my bare arms, feeling my skin, giving me chills.

"Then, why are you here?" he asks, hopeful but confused.

"Because I realized you're right about who I am. You're right about what we have. It wasn't just on the island." I reach over and take his hand, pulling it to the top of my breast, over my heart. "It's here. I realized that I love you, too. I don't want to live without this." I press his hand even harder on my chest.

"Good." He steps in, bringing our bodies flush together. "Neither do I." He holds me and asks, "All of you? I get to have all of you?"

"Every last little bit inside of me is yours."

Our mouths open, and we connect. He kisses me, and it's unlike any other kiss he's given me before.

This is a kiss worth surviving for.

When our lips finally part, I ask, "Now what? Where do we go from here?"

Guy brushes a strand of hair away from my eyes. "Anywhere with you. I don't care if it's the middle of Manhattan, on a plane, or in the middle of a deserted island. It doesn't matter as long as we're together."

I breathe out, finally feeling content in his arms. "All that sounds nice, but maybe we could settle for The Plaza for a few nights?"

He grins and nods. "Yes. I'll get you that five-star resort you've been craving. Anything for you, Nay."

# Epilogue

## One Year Later

I walk up behind Guy, draping my arms over him as he muses over the documents on his desk. I look ahead, outside his office window, and admire the misty morning. The fog is settled just above the tree line, enough for me to see the dark green leaves and thick branches that part at the start of our hiking trail.

*Our* hiking trail.

When we searched for our house, we knew we wanted to be surrounded by nature and secluded, far away from the lights and bustle of New York City. But also not too far since I still have my nonprofit, and Guy still has his company, which is thriving now more than ever.

"Beautiful view." I continue to admire our Connecticut acreage. It's no deserted island, but it's our other slice of heaven on earth since we've been rescued from our island.

Guy twists his neck around to see me. "Now, it is."

Our eyes meet, and our smiles broaden.

I gently kiss him on his smooth, groomed cheek. "The last of the furniture should be delivered in about a half hour. I just got a call from the driver."

"No time for a run then?"

"After." I kiss his lips this time.

He turns in his chair and guides me onto his lap. "I need to keep you in shape."

I chuckle. "Oh, I think you do a pretty good job of keeping my heart rate up."

That hunger in his eyes returns—the one that means he wants to devour me. He leans into me, and I lean back, teasing him.

"Maybe my wife needs a little exercise right now?"

I stand up and back away. "There's no time for that." I know exactly what he means by *exercise.*

He stands, too, and takes a step in my direction. "Mrs. Harrington, you're the only woman in the world for me. There's always time for you."

I laugh and continue to back away toward the open office door. "Not according to our delivery driver. And I told you," I playfully scold, "don't call me that."

He nears me as he says, "Remind me, why is that again?"

I can hardly get the words out as I laugh. "It's too formal, Mr. Harrington."

His eyes spring open wider, and I know he's ready to pounce on me. I turn around and run out the door.

"Oh, now, you're going to get it." He takes off down the hall after me. "I told you never to call me that."

Once I reach the end of the hall, there's nowhere for me to go but into one of the rooms. He has me trapped. I squirm and giggle with my hands in front, begging him to go easy on me. I back up into a corner, and his body becomes more relaxed as he cages his arms around me.

"There's nowhere you can run where I won't find you."

I laugh and throw my arms around his neck. "I know that, but the chase is still fun, isn't it?"

His hand slides down my side and around the curve of my lower body. "It's all fun. Each and every day is an adventure."

I can feel my smile fade, and the adrenaline I was feeling is replaced with nerves. "We're about to have a pretty big adventure. Are you sure we're ready for this?"

Guy's expression becomes serious. "We can do anything, Nay. I know we can do this."

"I know. But two kids? It's such a big responsibility. I want to make their lives better, but I'm so scared I'm going to screw it up."

"Hey," he grabs my full attention. "You're stronger than you think. Two will be nothing for you. We've got six bedrooms and six thousand square feet. We could adopt six kids, and they would each get a thousand square feet."

I begin to laugh again. "But there'd be no room for us."

His fingers go under the hem of my dress and press between my legs, making my body pulse. "I'll find room here."

"Oh my gosh." I swat his shoulder. "You're incorrigible."

"I'm hopeless when it comes to you."

I look into his eyes, feeling more serious. "You're going to be a really great dad."

"You're going to be a really great mother."

Looking around, I realize something and say, "Soon, this room will be filled with a crib. It won't be just the two of us anymore."

His eyebrows rise. "I'm well aware. Instantly, we'll be a family of four. It's nothing we can't handle."

"I know." I muse. "Deep down, I really know that. We're lucky we were able to find siblings to adopt together. It would have broken my heart for them to be separated."

"See?" He smiles. "You're already a great mom."

I step back from Guy, looking around, imagining how the furniture will fit in the layout. "The crib will go here." I point. "He's almost one, but he'll still need a crib for at least another year."

Guy follows my gaze and nods.

I move to the far corner. "And here is where the rocker will go, and the bookshelf will be next to it, so we can read to him and rock him if he has trouble sleeping."

"Perfect," he agrees.

I take his hand and lead him to the room on the other side of the hall. "And Savannah's room, I've got it all planned out. She's only three, so I got her a toddler bed." I look at Guy. "You know, the one with the rails, so she doesn't fall out. But, hopefully, she'll be excited about having a big-girl bed." I start to feel nervous again. "You know, I just decided on pink, thinking that all little girls like pink. But I don't even know what her favorite color is. Maybe she'll want a purple bedspread."

Guy pulls me into him. "Then, baby, next week, when we meet her, we'll ask her what her favorite color is, and if it's not pink, we'll order a different one."

He's right. I have a tendency to complicate things. My arms move around him, and I press my body against his.

"How would I ever survive without you?"

"You wouldn't," he simply says and then kisses me.

But our moment is interrupted by the sound of our doorbell.

We smile at each other, knowing our home is about to be filled with our children's furniture.

"Ready for the ultimate adventure?" Guy asks.

"With you? Always."

# Acknowledgments

This book was fun to write … but it wasn't easy.

I feel this need to constantly push myself. That's why my books are all so different from each other. I'll never be an author that fits a mold. So, with that said, I wanted to challenge myself to write about sex. I wanted it to be raw and realistic but also magical and powerful. I've never written about sex so boldly in my other books. It wasn't easy, but like all challenges you face head-on, it felt good!

If it wasn't for Jovana Shirley with Unforeseen Editing, I'd be terrified to publish anything. But it's because of her skills and talent that I feel confident in sharing my stories—no matter the genre or topic.

At first, when I came up with this story for *Justified Temptation*, I thought it was so cheesy. But there was such a deeper meaning behind it for me that I had to share. What I get the most out of it is that it's fun. And that's what I want my readers to experience—a fun read.

Speaking of fun—nice segue :)—I never realized I could have so much fun in my late thirties. It's all because of my amazing friendships that have formed into a solid foundation of trust, respect, love, and, yes, fun.

> Amanda, I love you so much! You're so supportive. I'm not sure I could do this author thing without you. You have brought so much to my life, and I value every minute we spend together and every call we have, which is every day. I'd be lost without you.
>
> Dani, my Dani, how is that that we can be moms and married and have career ambitions and go out for long walks in the middle of the day, talking and talking and talking until our legs fall off? We laugh, we cry, we have deep, meaningful conversations, and we have conversations that make me smile, just thinking about them. I feel like you *get me.* Just being with you teaches me so much about myself … and also, I learn a lot of big words.
>
> Danna, you're such a breath of fresh air to me. I love how we have so much in common. I feel so grateful that you actually like me because, if you didn't, I'd probably know it. You live unapologetically—and you're wise beyond your years even if you'll look fifteen forever—and it's what I admire most about you. That, and our mutual love for pedicures, purses, shoes, wine—all things girlie. I love how you went on the internet and found the purse you knew I was picturing for Naomi. But then we also share this competitiveness. I cannot wait until we have our all-night poker game. You're going down!

I've found beauty in my friendships, and I can see the depths in each one of them—not unlike a book. There's so much here. And there's so much that needs to be written. I'm trying my damnedest to get it all down on paper.

I feel like I'm able to appreciate all these friendships and relationships I have now because of the great one I had while I was growing up. Tara, the memories I have from all our adventures are ingrained in my mind. If you ever forget, call me because I remember every laughter and every tear. I love you, and I love that there are so many more memories for us to create. And, if I ever need a little extra boost of inspiration, I just look at you and all you continue to accomplish. Letove yetou.

Where would I be without my husband? I'm obsessively in love with Phil Lockwood. And those eyes! If you've met him, you know what I'm talking about. I am so grateful for all the love in my heart for this guy. I've learned that, if you give love, you receive love. And there is a lot of love in our marriage. Once you realize happiness is a choice, so many things that have always felt hard will become easy. That includes marriage. I feel like I can just sit back and appreciate him for who he is, and he is incredible. I've never met someone who can just decide he wants to do something, no matter how big of a challenge, and he can just make it happen—simply because he decided to do it. I'm so lucky to be a part of it all. I'm so lucky he loves me.

I have so much support in my life, but what really touches my heart is the support I get from my readers. Some of you had never heard of me when you decided to read one of my novels. Thank you for taking a chance on me. And some of you have read my books because someone else recommended it. Thank you for trusting that person and reading my stories. No matter how you came across this book, no matter what you think of it, thank you for picking it up and reading it. I love writing and storytelling. It's my life's mission to spread that joy.

# About the Author

Erin Lockwood is a psychological fiction author for readers who seek an emotional connection with surprising plots and familiar characters.

She simultaneously offers original and relatable stories that stimulate the mind and captivate readers with both tragedy and insightful enlightenment, leaving them with "all the feels."

After growing up in Castro Valley, California, Erin attended the University of Oregon where she graduated in 2003 with a degree in journalism. From there, she moved to Denver,

Colorado, where she found the love of her life and built the family of her dreams.

When she's not gushing over how gorgeous her husband's eyes are, she's watching Oregon football, daydreaming on Coronado Beach, or mentally choreographing her performances for *Dancing with the Stars*. Because, after all, that's her end game—to someday win that Mirrorball trophy.

Learn more about Erin at ErinLockwood.com.

Made in the USA
Columbia, SC
30 June 2018